Jesus and the Adman

RHIDIAN BROOK

Jesus and the Adman

RHIDIAN BROOK

Flamingo
An Imprint of HarperCollins*Publishers*

Flamingo
An Imprint of HarperCollins*Publishers*
77–85 Fulham Palace Road,
Hammersmith, London W6 8JB

Published by Flamingo 1998
1 3 5 7 9 8 6 4 2

Author's Note: No characters in this book are
based on real persons, living or dead.
The advertising slogans, jingles, headlines etc.
are all fictional, too.

A catalogue record for this book
is available from the British Library

ISBN 0 00 225758 0

Set in Meridien by
Rowland Phototypesetting Ltd,
Bury St Edmunds, Suffolk

Printed and bound in Great Britain by
Clays Ltd, St Ives plc

For Nicola

Timor mortis conturbat me.
(Fear of death disturbs me.)
DUNBAR

For every fear there is a product.
ADVERTISING MAXIM

PART ONE

Contention Gets Attention

ONE

He needed a good line. The right words, in the right order, with the right rhythm and resonance could make the difference between success and failure, between renting a flat in Morton Road or owning a house in Park West Gardens. He just needed seven or eight words to transform an average marmalade into the most desired conserve in the land.

He held the bevelled jar up to the light, turning it slowly in his hand, looking for its genie. He could see the rind suspended in the jelly like plankton in a fiery sea. This was, according to the manufacturer, a very thick-cut. How had the brief put it? 'Madrigal is for people who like to *see* oranges in their marmalade.' He checked the ingredients and saw that oranges came third in the order. He noted the label with its simple orange tree motif and the pretentious script of the maker's name.

The lid told him that he'd best eat the product before December 1999. He twisted it carefully lest the genie slip away with its secret. He sniffed and there was almost a smell of oranges – oranges and something like alcohol. He scooped a lump onto his toast, spread it to the four corners and ate. He detected the gumminess of the pectin then the sweetness of the sugar spread across his tongue.

He waited for words to stir.

Conserve, reserve, preserve, deserve.

He swallowed some more in the vague belief that eating the product would yield up its essence; that through

3

some process of absorption the right words would distil and rise from his stomach to his mind.

Peel, pith, kin, skin.

It was, of course, just a jar of marmalade but it contained the essence of his future. In that jar, in the jelly, in the rind, somewhere, there existed a phrase so sweet that it would capture the minds and hearts of all who read it. A line that would become part of the national consciousness; words that would help make his mark in this world.

It would be hard to distinguish Madrigal from the other forty brands of thick-cut marmalades on the market, but it was his job to distinguish it, to mark it apart from all the others and convert the doubting, indifferent, ignorant marmalade-eating public to its ways. It didn't matter that it tasted no better than any other marmalade. He had to imagine that it did and make others believe it, too. To be good at this game he had to find absolute faith in this product; believe that it was the only marmalade worth buying. He had to ignore the fact that there were a dozen other marmalades made with finer oranges, brighter labels, or smarter jars. He had to tell them that Madrigal was special. A bright, shiny lie was better than the dull, blunt truth.

Come on. I know you're in there. Come out you sharp, sugary conserve-selling phrase. Talk to me now. Give me the words. One good line. Just one good line.

But for now the line, if it was there at all, remained conserved in the jar, denying him, and as he put the lid back on he thought he heard it sniggering:

What are you going to say about me, No-Lines Johnny? Are you going to tell them that I taste just like all the others? That I don't represent good value? That my only redeeming feature is misleadingly classy packaging?

He replaced the lid to silence the taunts and proceeded to eat his breakfast. The back of his cereal packet suggested that oats eaten regularly would help him live longer. He could believe that. Partly because he knew that oats were good for a person, and also because he wanted to. He wanted his life to be as long as possible. There was much to do, see, feel, eat, touch and sell and he was prepared to swallow anything that promised him such a thing.

As Johnny Yells set off for work he recalled the words of Wollard, his boss: 'An adman must be vigilant. Inspiration for a line might come from the unlikeliest source: a snatch of conversation, the smell of something you eat, or a half-read story in a newspaper. Treat everything as raw material. Immerse yourself in the product and it will begin to speak to you in every little thing that you do,' he'd said.

And it was true. As Johnny looked the leaves seemed golden orange on the trees and those that had fallen lay like rind on the pavement; the traffic lights blinked amber and the terraced houses of Morton Road were racked like toast. The people flowing towards the station all walked with their heads bowed, their minds on the day ahead. How much happier they might all look had they started the day with Madrigal.

He crossed the road by the Fox and the Grapes. Like the fox in the sign, he was still striving for the grapes, needing to make a difficult leap to get to the juicy fruit. He would not give up until he had the fruit in his mouth.

At the newsstand he stopped to buy his paper. Raw material. The vendor was chanting his daily refrain: 'Bad news: come and get it.' He slid Johnny's paper from its stand, folded it and took the change in one motion. When Johnny suggested that bad news was good news for him, the vendor answered him with a gloomy assessment: 'I don't know where it's all going to end, but it is going to end, that's for certain. And when it does, there won't be any people to write the news or people to read it.'

The century ending was working people up into a state

of gloomy prediction. Naturally Johnny kept a professional eye on any trends in public mood. Advertising agencies had to monitor and respond to such things: his own agency had just produced the Shapiro GT commercial in which the car raced across a red desert pursued by the Four Horsemen of the Apocalypse. 'The Shapiro GT: it's a hell of a drive.' But such tensions were not getting to him personally. His future stretched away, a clear, straight road to the next century.

On the platform he squinted at the paper which always connected him with the world and made him feel a part of it; but as he stared at the grave headline above a burning building the event seemed obscure and distant and far less urgent than his need to advocate an average marmalade to an entire nation. The paper's headline only reminded him of the lack of his own.

Across the track, on the opposite platform, there was a large poster for the Fly Express Train. 'Catch it if you can,' it said. The insect-front of the Fly Express travelling at one hundred and fifty miles per hour blurred so that it did indeed look like a fly. Johnny scrutinized the copy, looking for any unnecessary alliteration, puns or overstatements; he asked himself if it held his attention and sold the product well. He had to concede that the image worked well with the headline but he told himself that he could do better.

He paced the platform. Oh yes. He could do better. There was nothing like competition to galvanize his creativity.

Madrigal Marmalade: Break your fast.
Madrigal Marmalade: for a fruitful life.
Madrigal Marmalade: a cut above the rest.

On the train he pulled out a novel from his case and absently read the first paragraph, but he could not enter its world or stop himself from reading the advertisements in the strip-lit sections above the seats. Other people's lines distracting and challenging him.

An advertisement for a shampoo called 'Rain' showed a woman leaning over a balcony in a tropical country, her hair clean and bright and luxuriant and liable to make any other girl feel inadequate and bereft without 'Rain'. She looked from beneath a canopy onto a blackening sky whilst a man looked admiringly at her shiny hair. 'Looks like Rain,' said the line. It was a good line and Johnny felt the queasy pleasure that mixes appreciation and envy. He had yet to see one of his own efforts on the journey to work and it would take a line as good as that to fulfil that ambition.

Two women in the carriage started talking about flu. Johnny listened to their hushed, weary tones. One of the women was wearing a coat that was a little early for October and she sniffed and coughed her complaint to her neighbour who humoured her with reassuring platitudes about there being 'a lot of it about'.

Flu, vitamin C, oranges.

Could Madrigal claim medicinal benefits? *Madrigal Marmalade: zest for life.*

At his stop he hung back to avoid the buffeting and shove of the crowd. He let the tide of people move up the stairs ahead of him and walked slowly, trying to squeeze a line from these last few seconds before getting to work.

Rush, crush, oranges. Come on. Think.

At the top of the stairs a man with a sandwichboard was blocking the route to the escalator. He had positioned himself in such a way as to make it impossible to avoid passing him or his placard. As they approached him, the people ahead shuffled as far over to the right as they could, buried their chins in their lapels and quickened their step. The man declaimed at them all the same, his words falling on stony, deaf ears. 'You can wear that dress madam if you like,' he said; 'you can wear whatever you like. And you too, sir. It doesn't matter what you do, who you are, what you've done. You're all welcome.'

Johnny hugged the wall and looked down at his feet as he reached the top of the stairs. But the man had moved to the centre of the alley and the words on his placard, painted in a wobbly white on a black board, confronted him: 'In heaven there are many mansions.'

Given the man's aneuritic skin, sunken cheeks and general lowliness, it was easy to see why he would wish for such a thing. But for Johnny, these words fell as flat as a badly targetted, ill-timed advertisement for a product no-one wanted.

'He's got a mansion waiting for you too, sir,' the man said, looking directly at Johnny now. 'If you want it, that is.'

'That's nice,' Johnny said, absently, his mind still juggling muddled ingredients.

Mansions, palaces, kings, serenade, madrigal, marmalade.

No doubt the man thought he was a sage communicating some vital truth that had got lost in the to and fro of this rushing life, but he was ruining Johnny's train of thought.

'You just have to accept Him,' the man went on undeterred by the indifference.

'Right,' Johnny said. He couldn't begrudge this man's need to believe in such things but he hadn't the time or the inclination to stay here and discuss eternal destiny with him. He raised his hand in a gesture of 'no thanks'. But the man took a step forward and tapped his board. 'He promised us. Now He wouldn't have promised us if it wasn't true, would He, young man?'

Young man, old man, ripe fruit, rotten fruit. What are you doing standing here listening to this? Leave him to his delusions.

'Trust His word,' the man said.

'No thanks. Please. I have to get to work.'

There might be a life after death, there might even be mansions there; but Johnny wanted real, not fictional estate. As he bounded up the escalator towards the world, he could still hear Scripture being muttered at his back. He was glad to reach the exit where the reassuring hubbub of the city drowned out the man's words. Thankfully, Johnny had a roof over his head, a happy balance of chemicals in his brain and something believable to sell to the world.

TWO

The building that housed WWW Advertising was designed to intimidate rather than welcome its visitors. There was an air of cool triumph in the facade and a stark minimalism to the decor in the foyer. If the building could talk it would use short, clipped sentences, and occasionally look away as if addressing someone more significant.

Above the stainless-steel, bullet-shaped reception desk three Ws formed a triptych, the letters joined to give the impression of a boxer having his arms raised by his two trainers who were themselves raising their arms in triumph. The sum of these initials exercised a curious power in the world of advertising far greater than the parts. No-one could actually remember who the original Ws were, an ignorance which led to conjecture as to what the acronym stood for. Winning (more awards than any other agency in the last ten years); Wonderful (how its employees felt about working for the company); Wealth (the highest billings in the industry).

Johnny always felt slightly startled that he worked here. He had that same sense of awe that acolytes must have felt walking the cloisters of a cathedral. In this place he was in the company of some of the most creative and talented people in the land and he was counted as one of their number.

And what talent. The evidence for it was all about him. See the Gold and Silver Plaques covering the walls – the awards that the agency had won. 'Look at us,' they sang,

(the Gold the melody, the Silvers the harmony). 'We
have done great deeds in the field of creativity. A winner in every category, in every year for a decade. Who
else can put on such a display?' No Golden Plaques
for Johnny yet, but it was just a matter of a line;
just a matter of time before his good ideas turned to
gold.

Ideas: the currency of the agency, the precious and
essential material of the creative adman. A good idea
breathed life into a lifeless product, made it sing and
dance; it was the bait in the trap, the cheese that drew
the mousy in to trigger the snapping metal and close the
deal. It didn't matter where they came from, just as long
as they came and came consistently. Without ideas an
adman was a deadman.

Johnny bade the receptionists hello. They nodded
reluctantly as if fed up with greeting every employee
that passed through. By some architectural osmosis they
adopted the cool tones of their surroundings. They were
often peremptory and contemptuous, answering queries
as though they were being interrupted in the middle of
a task far more important. Such disdain might have
seemed foolhardy in the reception desks of lesser agencies struggling to make an impression, but WWW had
earned its right to haughtiness.

Johnny walked past unseasonably green yucca, cheese
and spider plants and a fig tree that would never wither
in this ersatz summer-all-year-round climate. On and
into the cranium of the building: the Creative Department with its characters, its noise, its considered sham-
bolic look.

Despite its open plan, the Creative Department had its
hierarchy. At the far end, in the glass office overlooking
the park sat Wollard, the agency's imperious Creative
Director, author of several nationally-known catch
phrases, recipient of a record ten Golden Plaques. Johnny
could see him there now, sitting on his swivelling throne

11

delegating and distributing, still wearing a tracksuit from his morning run.

Next in line, and just the other side of the glass partition, was Bill Andrews, a loud and aggressive pretender whose Golden Plaque for the Connoisseur Cat Food campaign had established him as the agency wunderkind, adding volume to his banter and strut to his walk. He was now recalling, with undisguised relish, his weekend's conquests whilst making himself coffee, a Monday morning confession that had become a ritual against which the interestingness of other people's lives was measured. The challenge was to make it to your desk every morning without letting Bill get in a quip at your expense.

Despite Bill's recent successes Johnny felt sure that he had more talent than the loudmouth. Every time he saw Bill's most recent campaign for Target Cologne, displayed on the wall behind his desk, he felt confirmed in this. The poster showed a woman looking back over her shoulder provocatively. She was naked and in the middle of her back there was a bull's-eye target. 'Target Cologne: for men who've set their sights.'

Next to Bill sat Taylor, the oldest in the department and a survivor of several regicides. His ability to ride the constant shifting of personnel had given him the seen-it-all air of the cynic. Taylor had established his reputation many years ago with the 'Give me time' jingle that had become as indelibly stamped upon the national subconscious as a nursery rhyme. Johnny had whistled that tune himself as a teenager and, ten years on, he could still recall the jaunty jingle word for word: *'Give me time, give me time, but make it Quartzaline. I'm on time, I'm on time, I've got Quartzaline.'* That was success, Johnny thought. Twenty words and your career secured.

A middle tier of creative teams was located in the centre of the room, vying for honours and agency immortality. Hutchen's and Brewer's desks were currently empty because they were on a shoot on a tropical island where they were trying to improve the dour image of a bank. They had come up with the idea of constructing several beach huts and a 'beach bank' distributing cash to sunbathers. It was all part of promoting the client as 'The Sunshine Bank'. Johnny did not begrudge them their exotic and profligate shoot. They would be away for two weeks and that meant that Johnny and his partner – Edson – were the team most likely to pick up any new briefs coming in.

Johnny was pleased to see Edson already at his desk, scribbling something – perhaps a line for Madrigal. He took off his jacket and sat down opposite his partner, noticing the distinctive Madrigal logo already sketched on Edson's pad. Johnny waited to see if Edson would write anything beneath it.

Bill eased over, looking for banter.

'We were admiring Eddy's beard, Yells,' he said. 'Thought it made him look a little more with-it. What do you think?' Bill stroked Edson's beard for him. He liked to ruffle Edson simply because Edson was difficult to ruffle.

'It covers his weak chin,' Bill said.

Edson's beard only made him look more out of place in this smooth-chinned company, Johnny thought. Whatever he did, he always managed to go against the cut: his clothes were not archly sloppy or carefully snappy; there was nothing contrived or self-conscious about his appearance.

He took the jibe gamely. 'A beard would suit you, Bill,' he said.

'Yeah, it would give you a maturity to go with your position,' Johnny said, feeling that Bill needed to be kept in check since his catfood coup.

'Talent before age, remember,' Bill said, stroking an imaginary beard.

'Immaturity has its advantages here,' Edson suggested.

'Look what it's done for Bill,' Johnny said.

'Steady, Yells. You almost sound old and bitter,' Bill sauntered off knowing that he had hit the spot. He was a year younger than Johnny but he was several thousand pounds his senior. And all because he had had the idea of a cat who thinks nine lives isn't enough to enjoy his catfood. How Johnny longed for a line of copy to buy him another life.

'How was your weekend?' Edson asked, continuing to sketch.

'Hectic,' Johnny said. 'We looked at flats. Penny is very particular: she wants the garden to be facing a certain way, the kitchen to have a certain arrangement. We're looking at another tonight. It's never-ending.'

'Where are you looking?'

'Park West Gardens.'

'You can afford that?'

It was a fair question – Park West Gardens was an expensive area for a young man to be buying his first home – but Johnny was piqued by it all the same. Innocently, Edson had picked up on the very issue that had distracted Johnny for weeks: the fact that he didn't have the money that he needed to live where he wanted.

'Better to pay that little extra to get what you want than live in a place that constantly feels like a compromise,' Johnny said. 'Have you got something for Madrigal then?' he asked, his tone implying that he already did.

'Just the one,' Edson said.

'Can I see it?' Johnny asked, not wanting to like it but needing it to be good.

'Just finishing.' Edson may have been a little out of place here but he always came up with the goods. Johnny was counting on him coming up with the goods today.

Edson handed Johnny his sketch. 'I had a go at a line but I'm not sure about it,' he said.

Johnny looked at the mocked-up advertisement and felt relief and then, a little afterwards, gall. Edson had executed the idea perfectly, taking the orange tree from the Madrigal label, embellishing it with fruit and writing the line below.

'Marmalade like this doesn't grow on trees.' It was sweet.

Damn him. It's perfect. But don't tell him. Remember: you're the copywriter. A small tweak will give you some claim to it.

'Great minds and all that,' Johnny began. 'It's not unlike my own line.' He pulled a professional scrutinizing face and studied the drawing closely. He wasn't really looking at it. He was thinking of Edson's perfect line and his own failure to come up with anything as good. But he did not betray his admiration. Instead he tried hard to change the line and so make it his.

'I think it should be "Madrigal Marmalade, full stop. It doesn't grow on trees,"' and he added, with expert seriousness: 'It gets over the exclusivity better.'

Edson agreed that it was better. He was not precious or possessive about his work; in fact, he had a hazardous generosity towards his ideas and often gave them away for others to enhance and embellish and claim as their own. It was well known that he had given Wollard the idea for the award-winning Presto Tomatoes commercial, but no-one, least of all Edson, was going to point this out. He had no talent for one-upmanship and was seemingly unaffected by the slings and arrows of office politics or the competitive expedient of the work. In an environment where good ideas were a passport to promotion such benevolence was dangerous but, for now, it had its advantages. They were a team weren't they? And that made Edson's ideas Johnny's ideas.

'I think it's almost there. I tell you what. I have to see "W" about something. Why don't I stick this under his nose?' Johnny asked, trying to sound casual. Edson waved him on his way, suspecting nothing.

With its ornate, rosewood desk, Golden Plaques and posters for advertising glories from Wollard's recent and distant past, the Creative Director's office was a shrine to his achievements. The awards for Presto Puree were already there, claimed and framed. According to Wollard, the dancing tomato commercial came to him whilst he was making a salad and listening to a programme about the waltz on the radio. The tomatoes, he said, would not sit still beneath his knife, instead they danced away across the table, wobbling a three-step. Hence the commercial in which the tomatoes danced in pairs in a nineteenth-century ballroom. And why were they dancing? Because only the finest tomatoes were selected for Presto Puree and if you were a tomato you'd dance for joy at being selected for such a prestigious comestible.

On the back of Wollard's door hung a linen suit ready for client lunches; on the desk there was a gold fountain pen poised somewhat self-consciously over a plain, white pad. Wollard scribbled all his ideas with this most coveted writing instrument. That was style, Johnny thought, although the pretence did not entirely escape him.

On top of the bookcase there was a set of glass ornaments placed in ascending order of size. They were fish, each one a different colour and species with its mouth open ready to swallow; there were eight in all and each fish was smiling, unaware that they themselves were about to be swallowed by a fish with an even larger grin. The largest fish had the largest grin of all.

Wollard seemed pleased to see Johnny. 'You have something for me?' He was still shiny from his morning run and his slightly thyroid bulging eyes made him look aquatic, almost reptilian.

'Good time this morning?' Johnny asked.

'Fifteen minutes,' Wollard said. 'Third fastest of the year.'

'I hope I'm that fit at your age,' Johnny said. It was risky overfamiliarity but Wollard seemed to appreciate the mixed compliment. In his closed-mouth grin there

16

was both friendliness and prohibition: compliment me yes, but be careful how you go.

'I wonder if you'll make it to my age,' Wollard said.

Johnny felt his heart leap a little. He held out the Madrigal scamp. 'I think we've cracked it,' he said.

Wollard had a routine for assessing ideas: he took a deep breath and sniffed for the quality like a master of wine; then he picked up his gold fountain pen and tapped it lightly on his top lip. It was impossible to judge his reaction from his face. The telling sign was the frequency with which he tapped the pen, and as Johnny watched he saw, with relief and then delight, that it tapped with increasing beats.

'It seems that you are finding form.' He looked at Johnny, still nodding. 'I would like you to sit in on a pitch that is coming up soon: for LifeGen. Make sure you are included.'

The telephone rang and Wollard took the call, suddenly becoming more animated. 'Trellis, you dog. Did you buy it? Hang on.' He cupped the receiver. 'You'll have to excuse me. I have some art to buy. Nice work by the way.'

Johnny left Wollard's office with the blessed idea, inadvertently bowing as he went.

THREE

'Once you move here, you'll want to live here for ever,' the estate agent said. 'Park West Gardens has the lowest sell-on in the city. People just don't want to move. And who can blame them? It's perfectly situated. Nice balance between peaceful privacy and accessible amenities. Twenty minutes in to Financial. And the security of knowing that prices here are set like concrete. It's as close as many people get to heaven.'

Johnny let the car's window down to see. In the sanguine light the estate agent's words seemed like absolute truths. The sun's slant was giving an equality to all property, making every dwelling seem an ideal prospect.

'You've got the park here. The leisure facilities. More trees than anywhere in the city. The lowest decibel reading.' The estate agent continued to work for his commission, not that he needed to. The natural advertisement of the light had already won Johnny over. His girlfriend Penny, who sat next to him, pressed up against the window, matching his desire, brick for brick.

'We have to live here, Johnny,' she said. 'Look at all these trees. Look at the way the houses are all painted different colours.'

Johnny juggled figures, his desire forcing the mathematics to work: Penny had her lump sum to put down as a deposit, but their combined incomes were not quite enough to see them into this leafy nirvana. They would need another ten thousand – a small sum in the scheme of things, but an amount that seemed for now as unattainable as a million. They could wait and see if the price would come down, but there would always be someone else ready to meet the asking price. He needed the solid fact of capital.

The estate agent drove slowly to allow for maximum appreciation; eventually he came to a stop outside a three-storey home, discreetly divided into three flats. '29 Clamber Road,' he said, as though it were the palace of a king and he their tour guide.

The building faced into the sun and its brickwork glowed and teased. The estate agent, confident of his wares, tantalized them with more superlatives. 'That front garden belongs to your flat by the way. Nicest garden in the road. It's also the oldest street in the neighbourhood. Come on in.'

Johnny divined a new strategy and calculation.

Talk to your father.

'See the trellising. The masonry and the fittings and fixtures are all restored to the original specifications.'

Ask him for the money, a loan.

'And there are the stripped and varnished floors – all treated.'

He'll have ten thousand. He must have.

The estate agent waved them towards the kitchen to demonstrate something. 'The kitchen has Electrajet and a Zed Fridge. Touch reflex.' He held his hand over the cooker's sensor pad to make the flame spout and a quick surge of fire silently spouted and then disappeared as quick as a tongue.

'To touch is to know,' Johnny said, quoting the Electrajet commercial. 'I know the man who wrote that very line,' he said. 'He lives near here – in The Mansions.'

The estate agent whistled. 'Very nice. You should be able to see The Mansions from the bottom of this garden.' He unlocked the French windows and they all walked out onto the lawn where a great oak had carpeted the garden in yet more gold. He began to explain the

19

dimensions and features of the garden which was enclosed within a picturesque wall, but Johnny didn't stop to listen; he scrunched purposefully across the crispy leaf carpet to the end fence and squinted up towards the ridge where he could see the multiple chimneys and the iron trelliswork of the city's most elite properties. Wollard lived somewhere up there.

'That's real estate,' the estate agent said, joining Johnny.

'Do you know which one your friend lives in?'

'It's called The Grotto,' Johnny said.

'I know it,' the estate agent said. 'Haven't actually seen it inside. It's got some unusual specs, that place. I think it's got a pond.'

From here the hidden homes cast a shadow of impregnability.

'How much do they go for?' Johnny asked.

'Million a piece,' the estate agent said, as though he was used to talking such sums. 'That's it there. The one with the dome.'

'Which?'

'Amongst those pine trees. The dome. See it?'

The dome could just be discerned rising above the solemn woods.

'Your friend, is he?'

'My boss.' Johnny felt a tug at his elbow.

'Johnny! We've come to look at *this* property.' Penny pulled him back to earth.

'Maybe in twenty years time,' the estate agent jested.

But, to Johnny, the difference from here to there looked to be more than a hundred years. Those great homes up on the hill shrank the dimensions of his own potential accommodation and mocked his small time, jerry-built ambition.

'You'll have to content yourself with two bedrooms and a fifty-foot garden,' Penny said.

Johnny turned away and took in the more achievable

reality of Flat One, 29 Clamber Road. It certainly matched his greatest expectations, even in the more fanciful requirements of garden, wooden floors and modern fitted kitchen. And yet even this modest, first home was just a little bit out of his reach.

Walking back to the car, Penny took his hand and squeezed it urgently. 'It's the nicest place we've seen. Johnny, what are we going to do?'

'I'm going to talk to my father,' he said. 'He has money.'

'You haven't seen him in ages.'

'That'll make it easier to ask him.'

They paused at the entrance to the front garden and took in the handsome proportions and setting of the could-be-home and they could almost see and feel themselves living there already. It just needed the key of ten thousand pounds to get them to the rooms inside.

'It's our age,' Penny said. 'The number.' She pointed to the brass 29 gleaming gold in the sun that was going down. It was a tenuous sign but Johnny needed some irrational encouragement to steel himself. He gripped her hand tight and swore a fiscal oath.

'I'll get the money,' he said.

All this time, the estate agent stood a little off to allow them this discussion; he was silent, instinctively knowing that his percentage was safe. Eventually Johnny turned to him and, finding strength in the shining 29, declared that they would be making an offer.

As he got back into the estate agent's car, Johnny asked if they could go to the station via The Mansions. 'I'd like to get a closer look at my boss's house if we could. Just to see.'

The car climbed the hill and at the brow levelled out into a curving, one-way boulevard, interrupted by sleeping policemen which had the double function of slowing vehicles to a safe speed and forcing their occupants to admire and aspire to the very acme of real estate.

21

'You work in advertising then?' the estate agent asked. From his tone it seemed clear that he believed advertising to possess a glamour of some kind.

Johnny said that he did, feeling a certain pride.

'I love the ads,' the estate agent said. 'Did you do that beer ad with the invisible man starting a fight in the pub? I love that one.'

'That was another agency.'

'Done any I might have seen?'

WWW had created many advertisements that the estate agent would have seen and read and heard, but Johnny could not (yet) lay claim to their authorship. He offered the Shapiro GT.

'The one with the horses. Great music. You did that?'

'My boss wrote that one, too.'

'He's doing very well on it.' The estate agent slowed the car at a towering wrought-iron gate. A tree-lined driveway curved privately out of view. 'Here's his house. Must be nice, thinking up ads.'

There was no name to indicate that this was The Grotto but the dome was clearly visible above the trees; close up, its scale seemed even more impressive.

'You don't mind if I take a quick snoop around?'

'Go ahead.' The estate agent had earned his week's commission. He switched off the engine. 'Take as long as you want.'

Johnny walked up to the gates and ducked beneath the eye-line of the security cameras. He swung up onto the waist-high wall which was also railed and he moved along the perimeter stopping to look, holding the bars and pushing his nose through the railing, much like a peasant peering in at a regal world beyond reach. Because of the trees he was unable to see anything of the house other than the dome. He sidled further along until he was able to see more of the house through a break in the trees.

'Pen! Here.' He gesticulated towards the car.

Penny tiptoed over, glancing nervously at the security cameras. She stepped up on the wall and looked in with him. Through the opening they could see the house, or rather the top floor of the house: the rest of it was sunk out of view as if constructed lower into the hill, submerged there. Johnny shuffled further along the wall but the house remained a half secret and he had to build the rest of it in his mind.

'Magnificent.'

Penny kept looking over at the closed-circuit cameras. 'Why so much security?' she asked.

'He has a lot to protect. He's got a big art collection. One of the biggest in the country.'

The top windows of the house were winking at them, the heavy glass pooley and taciturn, hiding depth but revealing little of what was inside. Any thief could see that those wine-dark windows promised treasures carefully discerned and heavily insured.

There was an ocean between him and such riches, Johnny thought. A great chopping sea with dark currents and lurking monsters waiting to swallow him whole. But he had the craft to get across it. It wasn't an impossible divide. With enough jingles and ideas, and phrases sweetly struck, he might make it. Wollard had done it, he had made his ideas concrete. Words to bricks, phrases to walls, lines to rooms. It was a pleasing alchemy. If a successful campaign could see him into the vicinity of Park West Gardens, who knows? Several award-winning campaigns, back to back, and he could move a little further up the hill.

There was a sudden animal rush and low growling, fast feet skipping. Through the trees Johnny could see the dark shapes of dogs. He jumped down and watched them come. The dogs leapt at the railings and pushed their heads through the bars, their shoulders just too thick to allow them further; only their heads poked through and snapped and flashed their bone-white teeth like evil cuckoo clocks.

The estate agent was finishing a cigarette when Johnny and Penny reached the car, their hearts beating hard from the encounter.

'See anything?' he asked.

'We saw enough,' Johnny said.

As they drove away Johnny looked along the wall again but the dogs were gone, back into the shadowed trees as if called by some invisible authority.

'Can't say I'd want to live in a place like that,' the estate agent said. 'Hell to maintain; think of the bills and the headache of protecting it all.'

Johnny did not say anything. These words were just the sound of someone kidding themselves, the platitudes of someone who had given up hope of ever moving on to something better.

FOUR

Johnny sat on the edge of a spongy airport chair looking out for his father among the weaving, ant-like movements of travellers. Of course, he knew what his father looked like but it had been a year since they had last met and the forecourt teemed with sober, purposeful businessmen – any one of whom might, at a sudden glance, pass for his father.

He guessed that his father was a successful businessman and concluded that he would, as any successful businessman would, have capital set aside for important moments in life: holidays, weddings, a deposit on his son's first home. And, given the distant formality of their relationship, it was as a businessman that Johnny had decided to approach the subject of the loan.

He considered his target audience: middle-aged male (mid-fifties), married twice, one child; professional accountant in the high income bracket (A1); financially prudent (not given to irrational spending); too busy to notice subliminal appeals. An establishment man with traditional values.

The tone of Johnny's pitch should be serious, respectful, and show business acumen and understanding.

Father, with your knowledge of the market, would you consider it wise to purchase a flat in a good area at a price that is some 20% lower than usual?

The seeking-advice approach had just the right mix of sense and flattery. What father wouldn't want to give his son financial advice? But maybe he should drop the

Father. Perhaps it would bring in an unwanted emotional element; any pretence at affection might raise the suspicion of a favour.

That was the hook. How then to phrase the request? The secret was to make the request sound like an offer, to make it seem that the loan was, in some way, an investment for his father.

With prices likely to rise in the next twelve months it would be a great shame to miss out on an easy and certain opportunity. Property is perhaps the most secure and sure way of making money. Ten thousand pounds will be fifteen thousand in twelve months' time.

As Johnny turned over the phrasing he wondered if perhaps the emotional approach were better.

I need you to help me, Father.

Just the plain, up-front request.

Father, can you loan me ten thousand?

Stripped of anything to dress it up the request sounded weak. Johnny could hear the 'no' and see the shaking head already.

A pale, pinched figure wearing a pained expression and a dull overcoat struggled through the crowd to Johnny's table. Confronted with his father's forlorn bearing Johnny wondered why he had imagined he would get such a large sum of money from him. This was not the face of a man about to bestow largesse upon anyone. Johnny had as good a chance of securing a loan from one of these anonymous travellers as he did from his father.

Johnny took his father's hand and was surprised by its coldness given the bothered beads of sweat on his father's brow. There was no hint of a bond between them in their greeting and had anyone had the time to notice them, they might have concluded that it was just another of the many working rendezvous that take place at airports. Indeed, Johnny felt just as though he was having an appointment with his bank manager.

His father did not look well, Johnny could see that. He was short of breath and it was some time before he was able to speak. Having sat down he glanced at his watch as if already begrudging the time that was moving too fast, as it always did for successful businessmen. When he did speak he was concise, as if he were preserving energy.

'I'm sorry that I'm late, Jonathan.' He signalled to a waiter.

'Water, please.'

'Still or sparkling, sir?'

'Tap.'

Johnny ordered a coffee and biscuits wondering how he was going to get ten thousand from a man who requested tap water and nothing more from a waiter.

'How was the meeting?' Johnny asked, remembering that his father had had to fit their own meeting in between meetings.

'It was three meetings.'

'That's efficient.'

'It was totally inefficient. One would have been sufficient.' His father was not being contrary, he was just being factually pedantic. He would never say what he didn't mean, a trait which would not suit him to advertising, Johnny thought.

The waiter brought the water and Johnny's father took a small white pill from a box in the pocket of his coat. He knocked the pill back with the water, returned the pill box to his coat pocket and managed a first, faint smile.

'To thin the blood. My doctor is telling me to look after my heart.'

Johnny pictured that tight, hidden muscle, seeing it pumping and straining to get the blood into his father's bloodless cheeks. He wondered if there would be a little space set aside in those constricting chambers for him; it would take the skill and precision of a surgeon to prise open that cold, blue place, massage some warmth into it, and get the rich blood flowing his way. Johnny's father looked at his watch again.

'You have something to tell me?'

'Actually I have something to ask,' Johnny began, brightly. 'Your advice.'

At hearing the word Johnny's father seemed pleased, as though a connection had been made. And this gave Johnny the confidence to begin his pitch.

'Penny and I are thinking about buying a property together. We have both been renting for the last few years and it seems that it's time for us to get on the ladder.'

The airport Tannoy announced some names and delays and Johnny waited for it to finish before pressing on with his little preplanned speech about the market, the timing, the bargain and the opportunity. He ended his pitch (which came out smooth and convincing as fresh, clear copy,) by asking his father what he thought.

'How secure are things with Penny?'

Johnny had anticipated this and in it he saw his opening. In comparative terms his relationship was going well; the first he had had that had lasted this long. It might not be love yet but at least their combined incomes would make it possible to purchase this property.

'We're both really committed to it. It'll be half and half. She has ten thousand to put down. Her father lent her the money. It seems safe and sensible for me to put the same amount down. And I was going to ask you if you might loan me the deposit.'

The part about Penny's father lending her the money was a little modified. She had, in fact, inherited the sum from an aunt, but if her father had lent her the money, why couldn't his?

Johnny's father looked at the table and Johnny

tried to catch his eye with a reasonable, questioning face.

'Father, I need ten thousand.'

The 'Father' was a radical departure from the business-like tone he had begun with. Johnny could not pretend that it was born from a sudden desire to begin intimate relations but saying it brought on an unexpected feeling of emotion and he leant back in the chair and sipped his cooling coffee lest he drop his professional demeanour any further.

His father did not say anything for a long minute.

'I am not asking you to give it to me,' Johnny put in. 'I just need the loan, for the deposit.'

Still his father considered. No hint of a yes or no, just a silent calculation.

'I can pay it back in two years. Perhaps sooner. Things are beginning to take off at work. I'm being given some big accounts to work on. Madrigal. The marmalade?' His father must have known the marmalade, maybe he had even had some at one of his conference breakfasts, but it did not register an impression.

Johnny looked around the lounge wishing he could point to an advertisement that he might claim as his own. Only a few weeks more and Madrigal might have been here; but what difference would it have made?

Loans from your father don't grow on trees.

His father looked suddenly pained again and Johnny took the wince to be a no. He could see the loan slipping away and with it the flat subsiding.

'The flat is a beautiful property. Park West Gardens.'

'Isn't that a little grand?'

'Yes, but that makes it a safer prospect. Property prices are set like concrete there.' The estate agent's words trotted out feebly here.

'You are in a precarious profession, Jonathan. You haven't been there that long. What if you lose your job?

29

And then there is this buying together. It is a big commitment. How long have you known Penny?'

'Six months. But we are committed.'

'To the property or to each other?'

'Both.'

'It seems a little rushed.'

Johnny could not prevent the pleading tone from seeping in. 'I can't pay rent for ever. How can I get started? In your day anyone could get a mortgage. It's different these days.'

More pearls of sweat were forming upon his father's brow. 'I will consider it in six months' time. When you have shown some commitment.'

'But the market could change and then I'll need twenty thousand.' His powers of persuasion could not unlock the steel safe of his father's heart.

'You said that you may get a rise. Why not wait until you have had it? Then you might actually be able to afford this property. I'll be happy to loan you the money in six months provided you have shown some commitment.'

Johnny could not effectively argue his case in the light of such logic. His father was giving him the good advice that he had been pretending to seek. He suppressed his frustration and smiled. Better to show his father that he had accepted the advice with grace and maturity and keep the long-term prospect of the loan open. In the meantime he would find the money from another source.

'You are right. I am probably rushing things a little,' he said.

His father took a sharp intake of breath and another sip of water. That white gleaming pallor and ill-tempered expression only made him seem mean rather than sick, miserly rather than prudent.

At the departure gate his father asked him to come and stay one weekend and Johnny said that he would.

They shook hands, his father seemingly intending some consolation in his look. Johnny watched him go, refusing to believe that the chance of buying his first home was flying away with him.

FIVE

Johnny lay on his bed staring at the ceiling while Penny read particulars for more garden flats in the west of the city. He was unable to concentrate for long on the prospectuses; after a time the properties began to sound indistinguishable: he could not picture the differences between a living room with French windows opening onto a south-facing garden and a kitchen-cum-conservatory that offered access to a patio area. Penny, however, continued to read with undiminished enthusiasm, determined to find new hope in the length and breadth of living rooms and the dimensions of bedrooms.

The pictures that she passed him at regular intervals somehow failed to match the adjectives used to describe them; he had a professional suspicion of adjectives; he knew how mendacious they could be, embellishing nouns, dressing them up, making them something they were not. 'Period' meant the flat wasn't new; 'characterful' meant it needed costly repairs; 'spacious' meant that it was large when viewed without furniture; the more adjectives used to describe them the less space there seemed to be in his head to picture them. And anyway, compared to the bright, elegant mansion that was 29 Clamber Road, Park West Gardens, these properties sounded like tight and airless boxes. 'Twenty by twenty-eight; fourteen by ten; a hundred-foot garden.'

Johnny looked up at the high and corniced ceiling and saw a thousand tiny cracks emanating like veins from the light fixture and a browning damp patch spreading in one corner. Someday someone would have to paint up there and he was glad that it wasn't him. The flat belonged to his landlord and friend Albert and those cracks were his responsibility.

'An ideal opportunity for first-time buyers to purchase a stunning garden flat in Uplands,' Penny said. 'It's in our price bracket.'

She passed him a photograph of the flat and Johnny saw what it was lacking rather than what it had. The flat was fine but it was in Uplands. Why should he compromise? He was committing to a twenty-five-year mortgage. He might live in this place for five of those years.

As he listened to the vibrations of Penny's enthusiasm, Johnny found his frustration redirecting towards her. He had always been attracted by her down-to-earth and matter-of-fact approach to life, her unwillingness to let things put her off her stride, but now it annoyed him. He wanted her to want 29 Clamber Road. He wanted her to believe that he could find the money they needed.

'This one has a fabulous living room. Johnny? Are you concentrating?'

'Yes, yes,' he said, clearing his throat.

'Are you all right?' Penny asked.

'I feel tired,' he said. He had a slight pain between his shoulder blades and in his sternum but he didn't want to admit to this.

'You're probably just stressed,' Penny said. 'It's meant to be stressful trying to find a home.'

He was angered at her cursory diagnosis. She wasn't him; she couldn't tell why he was feeling this way.

'I'll make you better,' she said in her baby voice. She began to caress his neck with her free hand. She was already naked beside him yet he could see no medicine in this. Nothing in him stirred except a gnarl of frustration in the core of his body: his very marrow seemed to ache with it, right down to the medulla.

Johnny thought of Wollard jogging through the city parks, keeping all bugs at bay; Wollard in his office taking and making calls, delegating, creating; Wollard in his vast house surrounded by paintings, some which were worth more than flats in Park West Gardens.

'I need to sleep,' he said. 'I have to be up early.' He turned away and pulled on his pyjamas feeling the relief of moving away from the light.

'We really need to find somewhere soon,' Penny said.

'I can't think straight at the moment, Pen. I need to sleep.' He pulled the covers up over his ears and left her to her prospects.

Later, as he lay on his side listening to the noises of Penny's sleep, Johnny thought of Edson and the line he'd claimed as his own in front of Wollard. He felt some remorse at this but he reminded himself that Edson was his partner and that this made his action acceptable.

Next to him Penny turned and made a grinding noise with her teeth before resuming her slow, deep breathing. She was in her own world, dreaming of fifty-foot living rooms backing onto two-hundred-foot, walled, mature gardens; all manner of fixtures and fittings: pelmets, wooden lavatory seats and restored cornicing.

How the sound of a sweetly sleeping person fuels the envy of the insomniac. Johnny worked himself up into a silent rage at his bedfellow's happy unconsciousness. That is, after all, what she was: a bedfellow: it was the bed that made them more than acquaintances, bringing them together in some unofficial way. Or was it her collateral? He recalled his father's question about how long they had been together, about his commitment to her, and as he lay there, unable to sleep from anger, Johnny knew that if someone had walked into the bedroom and said you must either marry Penny or go to sleep – you have ten seconds to decide – he would have left her. At that precise moment, he would gladly trade her in for a good night's sleep. Damn his father. Didn't

34

he know that his holding back on the loan would, if anything, make his relationship less secure?

He tried to think of nothing but nothing soon became something; his mind was not entirely his own, it behaved in its own way, wandering where it would. Previous girlfriends came to mind, relationships which at the time seemed eternally significant that now had a desperate transience about them. He tried not to think about his ex-girlfriends and in doing so he found them coming into his mind like a line-up of criminal suspects. So he let himself remember and then he indulged a memory or two and wondered if he had been happier with other girls.

By three, still conscious of the walls of his room, he began to find the soft corridor to sleep. He hovered at the door for a time, aware of himself, his heart and the soreness in his throat; and then he slipped away to dream a long, limpid dream.

He was house-hunting with a girl – it could have been Penny although her features never revealed themselves. They had property details in their hands, rolled in scrolls that were sealed with wax: the girl carried these while his own arms were free. They walked upon a plain with high corn grass and there was a wind because the grass was parting as though being combed. Ahead of them, on the rise, there were houses although to call them houses was to do them an injustice. They were mansions and they were evenly spaced across the plain, each with its own very particular style of construction. The first they came to (the one they had come to view) was colonial in style with clapboard sidings, a balcony and a veranda decked with rocking chairs. It was vast and Johnny (it was him) was amazed that he could be viewing such a magnificent abode. The quality of light in the mansion was startling: everything shone with a luminous clarity and outline. He was then met by Edson who directed him (the girl must have been left behind) into the mansion with a welcoming sweep of his arm. As he stepped in Johnny looked down at his feet and could not see them. He had no fear because the mansion had no floor. Inside, the rooms bore no proportion to the dimensions of the mansion as seen from the outside. He stood in a gallery that was oblong and the floor was of silver water and on the walls there were hundreds of paintings hanging and every picture was of a face and in the frames the faces were living, with the head framed as though the people were standing behind the frames. Johnny moved across the floor of water feeling nothing because he had no feet. At the end of the gallery he came to what must have been an atrium because there were birds, some of them flying high into a sky, others perching upon golden pedestals. The room itself stretched away on all sides to fabulously landscaped gardens.

Then the narrative of the dream changed and Johnny was in a running race with people struggling to get to the front. Wollard was there, pounding along, hardly breaking sweat, hardly breathing at all. Penny bobbed beside him, her hair in a ponytail.

Eager to show how fit and fast he was, Johnny pushed ahead but the pace was impossible to maintain. Inexorably he began to fall behind the running pack. He slowed to a stop and began to cry, not for his legs that had failed him but for the mansion he had failed to purchase in the other dream.

SIX

Wollard stood at the window overlooking the park, blocking the light. He held a document which he flapped like a baton and conducted the eyes of all those in the room: Bill's, Taylor's, Edson's and Johnny's.

'Something special has come our way,' he said. LifeGen – the life assurance people – want a nationwide poster campaign to go out in January. It's a little last minute but I insisted that we be in on the pitch. There are two other agencies being invited to present ideas: Prestwick-Danville and Trumpet. They'll select the most appropriate campaign at the end of this month.

'LifeGen are the new boys in life assurance. They're regarded as being a little brash in what is a highly conservative industry – that's good for creativity. The brief is short but it has a surprisingly clear single-minded proposition: to get more people to take out life assurance policies by the end of the year. You'll see this word "differentiation" – they're keen on that. As far as we're concerned that means standing out from the crowd. It's essentially an awareness campaign. They want people to sit up and take notice. Traditionally, life assurance is hard to sell: it's dull and prosaic and people are superstitious – they don't like anything that makes them think about death. You've got to overcome these fears, reassure them, tell them they can trust LifeGen. The fact is, everyone can use a little life assurance. People either live too long or die too soon.'

Wollard smiled a world-swallowing smile. He was

speaking with his usual authority, bringing the necessary sense of urgency and hubris to the meeting.

Die now; live later.

Life assurance, assurance for life. Life after death.

Johnny jotted his thoughts down. Next to him Edson began to sketch a portrait of Wollard, finding his likeness in a few languid lines and then, in only a few more strokes, something of the Creative Director's essential character. It was such a competent and truthful simulacrum that Johnny began to fidget at the thought that Wollard might ask to see what it was that Edson was drawing. The drawing clearly showed the dark spark in Wollard's eyes, and the meanness of the mouth. And if Wollard saw those bulging eyes and the strange naturally plucked eyebrows that slanted up at almost forty-five degrees across the forehead, he might decide to remove Edson – and thus them as a team – from this pitch. Johnny did not want to jeopardize anything, not now. He leant forward to shield the pad.

Wollard was delivering the brief staring out across the park. 'At LifeGen they are keen to be more direct in their approach to the subject of life assurance. They feel that, in the past, they and other companies have been too "roundabout" in their appeals.'

The door opened without a knock and Judy, the office secretary, poked her head round the door. Meetings in Wollard's office were never interrupted.

'I'm sorry, but there's a call for you, Johnny.'

'Can't it wait?' Johnny asked, the interruption blanking an idea that had just been forming in his mind.

'It's your stepmother. She said it was urgent.'

Nothing could be more pressing than taking this brief.

'I think you should take it,' Judy said.

Wollard indicated that Johnny take the call.

Johnny took the phone in an empty office where Judy had redirected the call. She closed the door behind him.

Even as his stepmother spoke to him, Johnny was

turning over the ideas that were darting in and out of his conscious mind; even as his stepmother told him, in a strange, quivering voice, that his father had died of a heart attack, Johnny was still thinking about the campaign. And, curiously, the obituary tones of his stepmother mingled with these phrases and ideas, confirming them.

Life after death.

His stepmother clearly mistook his silence for shock and she attempted to soothe him with assurances, saying that his father had died instantly and painlessly and that he was now at peace. Johnny had a picture of his father's stopped heart and he felt for his own, still steady and slow-beating, and he was amazed at the unchanged rhythm of it. The news of his father's suddenly-stopped heart made little impression on the pace of his own.

'Johnny?' Are you all right? I know it's a shock.'

'Yes. Yes. I'm fine.'

'The funeral will be at his church on Friday. Just a small gathering.'

You'll have to miss a day's work.

He stood in the glass room, watching the to and fro, the getting on with it in the office and he saw that there really was no stopping for anything in this world; that there were no two-minute silences for the recently departed. The disengaged voice speaking to him seemed to be having a reaction that was out of place here. He was, in truth, more anxious to get back to the meeting than to dwell on his father's untimely death; and perhaps his hard-working, watch-watching father would have wanted it that way.

The call came to an end although he could not recall the last few words exactly. When he put the receiver down he stood and breathed, felt no turn or faint of grief come upon him. Maintaining a professional composure he walked from the room and back towards Wollard's office.

'Is everything all right?' Judy asked him along the way; she looked at him, expecting bad news.

'Fine,' Johnny said. He didn't want to mention the fact that his father had died; there was nothing to gain from this – except unwanted sympathy; he did not want the platitudes of condolence and commiseration. More importantly, it would only disrupt things; he did not in any way want to scupper his involvement in this project. If he mentioned his father's death someone might suggest that he be excused from the meeting and hence the campaign. He could not afford this. His father had already deprived him of one opening, he would not spoil another. He wanted to get back to the meeting straight away.

Wollard seemed glad to have him back.

'Ah, good. We were just looking at previous work for LifeGen. It was done by TTT.' LifeGen ads were passed to Johnny.

'Pretty awful, as you can see,' Wollard said. 'It won't be difficult to impress them.'

Edson looked at Johnny as if something were amiss. Johnny averted his eyes and focused on the ever enthusiastic Wollard, still feeling that the news of his father's death was like the report of a tragedy far away in a distant land that was of no personal import to him. He was not going to complicate things with emotion that he did not feel or conjure up a grief that was not there.

Wollard wound things up and as he did he looked at the group, and, in particular, at Johnny.

'This is a major account and I want this business; it will give a certain balance to our portfolio. I certainly don't want Trumpet or Prestwick getting their grubby paws on it – that would be sacrilege. Take the brief away, mull it over and do whatever you have to do. Let the idea surface and bubble up through the competing babble in your brain. I don't care what you come up with, just as long as the idea is pristine and shiny, and says "Buy me, buy me!" I encourage you to be a little off the wall with this, a little risqué. Let's spruce up a dull product. Remember, gentlemen: in this world contention gets attention.'

SEVEN

On the way to his father's funeral, Johnny thought about life assurance. Had his father made 'a precaution for provision' as the LifeGen brief had so neatly put it? Surely, as a prudent businessman, his father had taken out a policy of some kind. He must have wanted to provide for his family in the event of his death.

Perhaps there would be 'life' after his father's death; 'life', that is, in the form of a handsome payout to those that survived him.

After life, death; after death, life.

As the church came into view some vague reproach censored these thoughts. Johnny had not been to church since he was a boy and he was now indifferent to its half-remembered myths and arcane images. But it still had the power to reprimand his thoughts and instead of thinking of his inheritance he tried, for now at least, to focus on remembering the deceased.

But as he contrived to establish an appropriate memorial he found no materials to build one with. The memories of his father were as vague as his sadness. He hardly knew him, having spent very little time with him as a child – when he had been sent away to school – or as a young man – when his father had been a globetrotting executive with little free time. Johnny had learned, from an early age, to live a life without him thank you very much; he could not fabricate feeling.

The mourners were gathering in the dripping grey, forming a black bottleneck at the church gates. The church itself was, to Johnny's mind, a drab construction spoilt further by scaffolding which covered the spire. At the entrance a great poster board said 'Church Appeal Fund' and a cross two-thirds filled-in in red showed that sixty thousand had been raised towards the target of one hundred thousand. Some of the filled-in red was, he knew, down to his father's benevolence. Apparently, his father had, when not away on business, regularly attended this church, and contributed not inconsiderable but unspecified sums of money towards its maintenance and restoration.

Johnny's stepmother stood beneath an umbrella at the entrance flanked by two women in a consoling huddle. He walked towards her, a slow funereal step.

She was holding herself together admirably and Johnny could not help wondering if, like him, there was an outward show of sadness and loss, whilst inwardly a mild surprise at how little she really felt.

'Jonathan, how like him you look,' she said, taking his arm and walking with him up the path to the church. Despite her respectful widow's rectitude Johnny thought she looked very well; she had plenty of life left in her, ergo plenty of time to whittle away any inheritance that might come her way.

Inside there was discreet and respectful silence for nothing he could fathom; he only felt dismay at the recondite features and furnishings of the place: the little books, the fat cushions, the brass floor plaques; all the paraphernalia of religion; he thought it all very odd, very cold, very quiet and very uncalled-for.

As he listened to the service he felt a growing resentment. A bespectacled man, not unlike his father, gave an obituary about a caring, hard-working man who had done much for the community and, not least, for this church which he loved. The thought of those misplaced funds gave Johnny a little twinge in his belly as though a worm were eating away inside him like the worms waiting outside for his father's body in the just-dug pit of the graveyard.

What a waste.

He wondered how much his father had in fact given. Had that ten thousand gone towards these varnished pews or that tottering spire? Had his father shown the same hesitation in giving money to this church as he had done to his own son? Johnny could not see how anyone, least of all his thrifty father, could give away money to such a cause. It did not make good business sense. It did not make sense at all.

Outside, having followed the coffin, Johnny stood slightly apart from the waterproofed group so that he might actually see the coffin lower all the way to the bottom of the pit in order to monitor any resurrection or last-minute escape from the grave. He watched the box go down to the peculiar poem: 'I am the resurrection and the life, saith the Lord ... whoever liveth and believeth in me shall never die' ... and the raindrops on the brass trimmings twinkled like gold and disappeared.

Johnny tried to imagine the expression on his father's face when he died: did he have the pained look of a man who had unfinished business to attend to? or had he been glancing at his watch when his own vital clock had stopped? No doubt the morticians, with their oils and ointments, had reset his grimace into one of peaceful resignation. Had he gone into the casket with a trinket or two – like a Pharaoh gathering his treasures about him? Johnny had seen the Pharaoh's gold amulets and shields laid in the tomb at the museum, all left behind. Was all that steady accumulation a pointless waste of time? 'Almighty God, with whom do live the spirits of them that depart hence . . .' The vicar was up and away again, talking as though Johnny's father were not in fact there in that teak casket but in some abstract transit station, some heavenly junction. The vicar orbited the earth with his ethery talk and Johnny looked down into that pit and thought only of the buried potential treasure and the fiscal ghost that would haunt him should none of it come his way. Never mind God's will; what about his father's? Was the vicar smiling at him as the earth was tossed onto the coffin; smiling because his father had, perhaps in some ridiculous act of good will and desperation, left everything to this shabby church instead of to him and the roof that he wanted to put over *his* head?

These next-life promises seemed absurd as they collided with the material realities of Johnny's life. And he suddenly felt a little smug for the right thinking of his own unbelief.

After the service Johnny strategically hooked his stepmother's arm and walked her to the side chapel where the funeral party were to be served revivifying tea and sandwiches. He could not be certain as to whether the wet marks on her face were raindrops or tears. He himself could not even muster the faux tears of a crocodile.

'I have something for you, Jonathan. From your father.'

Johnny felt some hope. Perhaps his father had set something aside after all. Maybe, aware of his fragile heart and imminent end, he had seen to it that Johnny would get the money he had asked for.

As they entered the vestry she reached into her bag for the heirloom/inheritance/legacy/cheque and Johnny thought it odd that she should produce a black velvet box of the type used for housing wristwatches.

'Your father was fonder of you than he was able to show, Jonathan. I think he regretted that. He always felt he did too little for you.'

Johnny had never presumed at any depth in his father's love for him but he hoped that some measure of it might now be found in the exciting black box being proffered. He took it and opened it and there, in the inlay, lay his father's Quintet Classic wristwatch still ticking its little life away. It was a valuable, 'heirloom quality', timepiece, the kind only ever advertised in the glossy, upmarket magazines.

There is no finer watch than the Quintet Classic (so called because of the five winders and the five readings in five cities worldwide). It marries expert, precision craftsmanship with robust design for today's living; it's the businessman's watch par excellence. In life there are no finer marks of distinction.

Johnny took it from its case and slipped it on his wrist, clipping the gold plate strap without having to adjust it to his own wrist-size.

'He always wanted you to have it,' his stepmother said as though bestowing some matchless dowry. She watched him snap the clasp. 'You have the same build.'

Except for our hearts, I hope.

A relative interrupted them and Johnny's stepmother kissed him on the cheek and left him to contemplate the time and his denied riches.

Johnny went to fetch himself a cup of tea and was intercepted by the man who had given his father's obituary.

'You must be Jonathan,' he said, his breath smelling of sherry. 'My commiserations. I'm Don Hamilton – your father's partner. He was a good man. We're going to miss him around the office. He really helped make the company what it is today.'

Dutifully Jonathan listened to the hagiography, wondering if Mr Hamilton was talking about the man who had been buried today or some other man who was good and popular and caring. This occasion was prompting a reckless honesty of thought in him; he wanted to ask Mr Hamilton what he stood to gain from his father's death, checking himself by concentrating on his pearly teeth that must have had years of brushing with Brushultra.

Clean, clean, clean before you dream, dream, dream.

His first thoughts were beginning to feel like the truest

response to this death. This peculiar rite of passage was like some quirky show designed to distract from the reality of someone's nonexistence. He looked around and wondered if, like him, his stepmother, the vicar, his father's partner, were all making a pretence of grief when really they felt nothing but relief for their own continuing lives. They may have a notion of a next life, might even imagine his father to be enjoying it right now, but this life was the thing they were clinging to.

Johnny wandered back into the church, not wanting to talk to anyone. He stumbled upon the vicar taking off his robes, folding them with ceremony even though no-one but his God was there to see him conduct himself in such a way. Johnny trod stealthily so as not to be heard; he did not want to be alone with a man like that. But the hard floor gave his tread away and the vicar looked up and came towards him.

'I'm sorry that we didn't have a chance to speak earlier; it's Jonathan, isn't it?'

Johnny nodded.

'I wanted to say what a good man your father was. He was much loved. We will miss him.'

'You will obviously miss his benevolence,' Johnny said, deciding to voice his thoughts.

'We will. He gave very generously.'

He began to see what kind of investment his father had made, or thought he had made. He had made a down payment on the next life; invested in his future there; he had bought an eternal life assurance policy.

'When you say "at peace", do you mean peace as in peace of mind, or do you mean peace as in sleeping peacefully, unconsciously? I mean, is he conscious of his peace, do you think?'

The vicar ought to know, Johnny thought; it was, after all, part of his job requirement and here was a grieving son in need of answers. The churchman made a face as if weighing the seriousness and sincerity of Johnny's question, unable to ignore the faintly mocking tone but needing to respect the feelings of the bereaved.

'I believe he has the peace of eternal life.'

Johnny noticed a pile of fund-raising leaflets on the table. 'How are you going to raise the last forty?'

'We may eventually have to sell some of these,' the vicar said indicating the paintings in the nave.

There were three portraits of Christ. The first and largest was bland and triumphal, depicting a somewhat prim Jesus with a red beard. He was proud, severe and a little superior, dressed in battle armour and at the head of an army. Next to this there was an equally disagreeable depiction of an overweight Jesus ascending in clouds and on clouds, while below him people fell upon their knees. Everyone wore badly faded clothes that looked as though they had been washed for years with a cheap brand of washing powder.

'How much will these bring in?' Johnny asked.

'I have no idea. This is the valuable piece. I would be sad to see it go.'

The vicar walked Johnny to a third portrait of Jesus, painted in the style of an icon. This Jesus had a long face, wide humorous eyes, a deep all-knowing but calmly flat forehead, tousled and unkempt hair and his skin was translucent and luminous. It was striking for its excellence and the unorthodox expression of its subject – an almost joyful smile of recognition and acceptance.

Despite himself and his impatience to get away from all of this nonsense Johnny thought he saw something sympathetic in that face and some tacit appreciation for Johnny's own mistrust and antagonism towards the subject. Maybe it was just a good painting, but something beyond pure aesthetics connected in him; he felt a gentle shiver coursing up his spine and tingling at his cortex.

It was the smile. It seemed, even to Johnny, that there was some secret understanding of what lay beyond this life in that all-knowing smile. This Jesus looked like a man who had gone to the other side and come back, and the knowledge of that great secret could be detected in his smile like an excellent joke he could hardly wait to share. Johnny momentarily forgot where he was, caught up in a kind of reverie with this image. He read the inscription on the gold plaque in the frame out loud.

'He who believes in me shall have eternal life.'

'You like him?' the vicar asked.

Johnny snapped from his brown study. 'That's some claim, that he makes,' he said.

'It is,' the vicar said.

'I like the smile. I can believe in that smile.' It was a smile he could use. Maybe, in the face of this pale revenant, with his wispy beard, his mysterious grin and unbelievable pitch, there was the seed of an idea.

'Do you have any postcards of this?'

The vicar briskly went to fetch a whole pile from the porch. 'It's quite a well-known icon. Brings in many visitors,' he said, handing Johnny a selection.

'This one is fine, I'm not so keen on the other ones,' Johnny said, keeping the card of the Smiling Icon. 'Well, thank you. I must be getting on,' he said, offering his hand. 'It has been inspirational.'

The vicar, no doubt interpreting this in his own light, smiled gratefully. 'I hope you will find peace when the grieving is done,' he said.

But as Johnny strode back to his car he already felt peace. He offered up a little prayer of thanks to the air; thanks for the idea that had dropped down from on high; and he smiled the smile of someone who knows that they have had a good idea and that it will come to pass.

EIGHT

On his way to work Johnny had no need for newspapers, novels or other people's advertisements. Since his revelation in the church he had been beset by his own vision. It was so clear, so vivid in his mind, that he half expected to see the advertisements already displayed on posters at the station, in the strip lights on the train, and in the magazines of his fellow commuters. He could hardly wait to put it to Wollard.

A number of people offered their condolences as Johnny entered the department. He didn't mind, just as long as it didn't detract from the matter in hand. Secretly, he was glad that people knew why he had taken Friday off: the commiseration might work to his advantage. He could already see them thinking 'Look at Johnny. He went to his father's funeral last Friday and here he is first thing Monday; what commitment.'

When Edson arrived he looked at Johnny with heavy sympathy, attributing too much weight to his grief. That was the trouble with well-meaning people, Johnny reflected. They couldn't just let the dead lie; they had to raise them up again, concoct a kind of resurrection from their concern.

'I am sorry about your father,' Edson said, meaning it.

'Life goes on, Eddy,' Johnny said, and he injected true feeling into his glibness.

'Maybe you should take a bit more time off?' Edson suggested.

'And do what? Miss out on this opportunity? My father

50

wouldn't have wanted that, would he? Besides, his death has given me an idea. Here.'

Edson did not seem convinced by Johnny's lightness of spirit. He took the mock-up advertisement without looking at it, keeping his eyes on Johnny.

Johnny tapped the paper. 'Aren't you going to look? It's a little rough but you'll get the gist. I've got a picture of the image I want to use.'

When Edson did look at the rudimentary advertisement, Johnny reassured himself with the truth that many great ideas for ads underwent a mundane analysis, even dissent, before they flowered into campaigns.

'Here.' Johnny passed Edson the postcard and he studied it with interest.

'It's beautiful – where did you find it?'

'In the church on Friday. I thought he looked a little like you.'

Edson kept looking, silently.

'You do get it?' Johnny asked. 'Life after death? Something's wrong. What is it?'

'I'm not sure,' Edson said.

'Not sure of what?'

'It's clever. And it's funny.'

'But it might cause offence. Is that it? It's harmless; at worst it's poking a little fun. I'm not saying it's wrong to believe in Jesus and all that malarkey, I'm just cashing in on his claim. Making people sit up. Contention gets attention, remember? It answers the brief perfectly. It's an award winner.'

Edson continued to struggle to explain his objection. Johnny saw this equivocation as proof that it was indeed a fine idea. 'Let me run it by Wollard; see what he thinks,' Johnny said, losing patience.

'He'll greatly approve,' Edson said.

Johnny found Wollard leaning against the side of his desk, half sitting, half standing and gesticulating theatrically. He was engaged in lively discussion on the phone and the door seemed left open intentionally so that the conversation might be heard by everyone in the office. Wollard liked to let everyone hear how interesting his calls/life were and he motioned for Johnny to take a pew and listen in.

The Creative Director was haggling over the price of a painting and the figure involved was substantial enough.

'Trellis, you're a scoundrel. You know he's a novice. He'll price himself to oblivion before he's made a name. Seventeen, that is my offer.'

Trellis, whoever he was, seemed to be holding out for something more than seventeen but Wollard was having none of it. 'Yes, yes, juvenilia; but an artist has to earn that kind of approval. Now, if you'll excuse me I have to earn my money. Call me with your answer.'

As this was going on, Johnny looked at three paintings propped up against Wollard's desk. They were abstract oils, slightly baffling and faintly menacing. As he looked at the blood-red lines on the white canvas he began to see that all of them contained parts of the human anatomy. They were all signed by an artist whose name Johnny recognized.

'I see that you have been admiring my Friedmans,' Wollard beamed, slamming down the receiver. 'I'm thinking of hanging them here. The house is a little cluttered.'

'They're very good,' Johnny lied.

'"1, 2 & 3". His first triptych. They were the first paintings that I bought. Cost as much as a cheap second-hand car when I got them. But that isn't the point of course. So, you have something for me?'

Johnny handed over the sketch and watched the gold pen. A good line was a good line straightaway or not at all, and he was pleased to see the gold pen beating furiously within a few seconds of Wollard reading. Johnny handed Wollard the postcard.

'This is the image I'd like to use.'

Wollard held the card and his eyes and nostrils dilated.

'Hello,' he said. 'Where did you find this sweet fellow?'

'The original is in an old church in Granton – just off the Western Highway.'

Wollard turned the card over. 'I see. The Smiling Icon of St Nicholas.'

Wollard's expression finally began to register in his eyes, a venal pleasure came over him. 'Always good to have a winning smile selling your product.'

'Do you think it might offend?' Johnny asked, wanting to deal with objections now.

'Who could it possibly offend?' Wollard snorted.

'Christians?'

'Do they still exist?'

'What about Standards?'

Wollard smirked at the icon. 'Compared to what we've been sending them lately, it's positively wholesome. Oh yes, I like this. It has legs,' he said in his voice that made people feel that they were involved in great things. 'Why don't you go and see what you can do with this Smiling Jesus?'

NINE

Johnny Yells, Johnny Yells, brimming with ideas;
Johnny Yells, Johnny Yells, best adman for years;
Posters to the left, billboards to the right;
Johnny Yells, Johnny Yells; boost your sales.

After work, Johnny jingled himself to the gymnasium, pumped up with enough approval to lift the building itself. He had finally discovered the essential alchemy of the adman: the knack of combining the right words with the right image to maximum and timely effect. He felt like a scientist who had stumbled upon the simple and beautiful answer to a problem that would change his perception of the universe.

Johnny would remember today as the day when his idea was pinned up outside Wollard's office and admired by the whole department. He recalled Wollard's delighted beam – a priceless reaction. And Bill's face, the eventual smirk of approval. Then Taylor's telling silence. Only Edson had shown any dissent – but Edson had never had a good eye for what would sell.

The fact that the idea had come to him in the middle of his father's funeral merely underlined the truth of Wollard's maxims: there is no telling where an idea might appear; everything is raw material for the adman; the only sacred thing in advertising is a good idea.

His father was proving far more helpful to Johnny dead than he ever had alive. His death had provided the inspiration for the idea; and now it was providing the impetus for a visit to the gymnasium. Johnny certainly planned to stay alive a little longer than the sixty years his father had had. He was going to protect his own heart from any hereditary ambushes that might be lurking with a new fitness regime. His heart was, as the cereal packets told him every morning, the vital cog in the machine and he must take good care of it. He would not repeat the regimen of hard work and no play that had brought his father's heart to an abrupt and painful stop.

Johnny leapt the twenty steps to the neo-classical facade of the Body & Soul Centre, with its glittering faux diamond ampersand, and for the first time he didn't feel that the robed attendants were quite so ludicrous in the light of his heroic deeds. Had he not scaled Olympian heights of creativity? As he stripped down to change into his sports gear he wondered at the physiological benefits of his success, imagining already that his breathing was better, his whole system running in higher gear.

He attacked the exercise machines with his new manifesto driving him on: *You are going to be fit and fast and lean and finely tuned and competitive and better than ever before.*

After the treadmill and the rowing machines he walked to the weights feeling his heart beating strongly and purposefully, no sign of mis-stroke or murmur; just the faithful, life-affirming beat thumping a happy Morse: *Thank you, thank you, thank you for exercising me.* He pictured again his father's blue lonely unexercised heart issuing its final, fatal complaint.

All work and no play made Ted Yells a dead man.

He pumped the bars and felt the weight come down and demand something extra from his central chamber; he breathed deeply and felt the beat of his heart and the rising of the iron weights pumping in unison, as if he were an essential part of the apparatus. He could hear the pumped plasma rushing in the shell of his ears and he continued to ask his heart for a long and strong life.

When he came to rest he saw, through a sweaty mist, Edson standing among the muscle and metal. His partner waved to him through the clash and crash of pumping iron, signalling that he would wait until Johnny was done.

So, after a strange silence, Edson had finally come to his senses, Johnny thought. He has realized that this Jesus idea is a great idea after all and come to say 'I'm in.'

Johnny took a shower, feeling expanded by the exercise, hardened and sweetly heady – almost pure, as though his former sluggishness were washed clean away.

'You should try this some day, Eddy,' he said, joining his partner in the bar. 'Build yourself up a little; put some space between your nipples.' Johnny bought the drinks and raised his glass to toast the campaign that would make their name.

'Cheers.'

Edson met Johnny's glass furtively.

'So, you have come round, Eddy.'

'I wanted to explain . . .'

'You don't have to. I understand. You're not the only one who will raise that objection. It was probably a good thing you did.'

'I want to explain why I'm not going to work on this campaign.'

'You what?'

'I'm not going to be working on LifeGen.'

'Look Eddy, I respect your morals, but I think you're making a big deal out of it,' Johnny said.

'It isn't about morals,' Edson said, mysteriously.

He was halting Johnny's drive with an equal and opposite force.

'Then what is it about?'

'Some things are sacred.'

Johnny laughed but it was clear that his partner wasn't

joking. It was then that Johnny realized that Edson believed in 'all that malarkey': in Jesus, the life eternal, heaven and hell and all the oddness therein. Of course he did. That explained it: he had the gullible innocence that made it necessary to believe in such things. Faith took up residence in weak-framed beings, people like the man with the sandwichboard, people like his father, people like Edson.

Johnny became indignant. His belief in this idea was as great as any other sacred claims. Yes, some things were sacred: good ideas were sacred. At WWW the idea was God. There were no sacred grounds where a good idea was fit to tread.

'We've done far worse. What about D-Lite Spread? The things we said about that, the goodness, the healthy choice. And what about Madrigal? Do their oranges really grow on special trees?'

Edson nodded. It was true. He had been party to bogus claims, but for some reason this was different. In that feeble frame of his there was an unbudging steeliness.

'Remember what business we're in,' Johnny pushed. 'Everything is fair game if it sells.'

Still a serious silence from his partner.

'What is it?' Johnny asked. 'Afraid we might get struck down? Think you might lose your plot of land in the next life?' He began to remember the contempt that he had felt at the funeral. 'If there is anything Standards should object to it's the claim that Jesus gives you eternal life. Come on, Eddy. People aren't going to object to this. I know it might be true for you but most people don't take it that seriously.'

'If it's true, it's true for everyone, or not at all,' Edson said.

Johnny's heart suddenly lost its steady rhythm and he felt a weight like a bench-press upon his chest. It might have been the endorphin rush passing, the comedown after the exercise, but he felt lethargic and a stiffness in his back and in his neck and he wondered if Edson had put some kind of a curse on him with his serious words and looks. Johnny sat up straight and made circular motions with his head that cricked his neck.

'Well, you have to make your choice,' he said.

'I've made my choice,' Edson said.

PART TWO

The Meaning of
Life Assurance

TEN

In the first week of the new year, a striking and gently provocative advertisement appeared on poster sites throughout the city, turning the heads and raising the eyebrows of the sleepy and distracted commuters. As they looked up over the tops of newspapers and shifted from foot to foot in the nasty chill of January they were warmed by the smile of a familiar face and an offer that few of the other products on view could match.

The posters showed an image of Jesus who was smiling more than many people were used to seeing him smile and a headline that read 'For Life after Death, talk to LifeGen.'

The advertisement was, client and creators agreed, a happy mix of worldly cunning and spiritual know-ingness, salty enough to cause some contention, clever enough to win respect. And with winter breeding its virulent flus and the hope of Christmas already fading, the promise of life after death and the unusually winning smile of the icon brought some cheer to passers-by.

Before long, the 'Smiling Jesus' campaign was getting wide reaction: a piece in a national newspaper, a discussion on the radio and one significant complaint from a leading bishop. For a short time, the names LifeGen and WWW became the focus for light conversation and middling opinion throughout the city. All of which was good news for the client and the agency, and excellent news for the creator of the campaign.

No-one was enjoying the sound of the hoo-ha more

than Johnny Yells. With every mention of it Johnny's status was augmenting, his bright future cementing. And it was the very subject of his future that was to be discussed and rubber-stamped by Wollard over lunch at Le Côte St Jacques, one of the more opulent restaurants in the city.

It was a bitter day as Johnny travelled to meet his boss but, for now, the aureole of success seemed to be insulating him against the chill; while the winter was thick with depressing financial and meteorological forecasts, his outlook was summer itself.

By happy coincidence he stepped from the taxi opposite one of the very posters that had earned him the right to his lunch with Wollard. With things going well, Johnny was beginning to believe that events had an intelligible purpose, as though some unseen force were driving them. Even seeing this poster now seemed timely. Then again, it wasn't such an exceptional coincidence to find one of his posters here: there were several hundred of them posted on stations, platforms and bus stops throughout the city.

It gave him a thrill to see his creation in such a prominent place, and an even more profound flush of pleasure to see other people looking at it. There were four people at the bus shelter and one of them was quite definitely looking at the advertisement. Unable to restrain himself, Johnny walked towards the shelter. He feigned a look at the timetable, simply to make sure the man was looking at the poster. He knew this to be an indulgent and obsessive thing to do (had he been with someone he would have maintained a blasé distance from his success) but success was still a novelty and he wanted to draw it out.

The icon had reproduced well: the rich ochre and gold colours and that smart smile demanded attention. Johnny wanted to announce to the waiting people that he had created this poster, the one that had recently enjoyed attention in the national newspapers (it was a double delight to read the news he had made) and he was about to say something when a flicker of disapproval in the eyes and mouth of the man presently looking at the poster stopped him. Or was it disinterest? Had he got it? Johnny looked at the image himself wanting to see in that smile some reassurance. He almost asked the man what he thought of it but checked himself as he realized how ridiculous he was being: hadn't he had praise enough? Hadn't the advertisement done everything and more than was expected? Wasn't he already receiving envy-charged accolades from his colleagues and expecting to pick up a Golden Plaque from the Advertising Awards in a few months time?

Le Côte St Jacques was situated in a narrow and anonymous alley in the fashionable-to-the-fashionable part of the city. It was not the kind of establishment that had to rely on passing custom from the street and on the barometer of Wollard's appreciation there could be no higher reading.

Wollard was already there and he beckoned Johnny to sit and called to the waiter all in one unbroken, mannered gesture. He looked comfortable here in the obsequious atmosphere of the restaurant, handling the waiters with a studied mixture of bonhomie and authority.

'Have you been to the St Jacques before?' Wollard asked.

'No.'

'There are, in life, some things that do not need advertising,' Wollard began heretically. 'Art, natural beauty and this restaurant. It has a kind of reputation that no hyperbole can taint. It's a rest for us who spend our days praising crap. There is no challenge in singing the praises of perfection.'

Johnny acknowledged the wisdom with a slow, attentive nod, like an apprentice to his master.

He tried to relax. Some phlegm was caught at the back of his throat, tickling him into coughing but he didn't want to cough in front of Wollard so he drank some water and cleared his throat. He must get used to the trappings of success soon in order to show that he was destined for it.

He tried to select a starter from the foreign menu, failing to recognize any of the dishes. In a ruse to flatter his boss and hide his ignorance, Johnny let Wollard choose for him. Wollard lived on a regular diet of flattery and when starved of it he became testy and liable to sack people. He held the menu and recommended starters as though they were old and trusted friends. Then he leaned forward and looked with histrionic pride at his protégé.

'How does it feel to be the bright light in the firmament?' he asked. 'I can't get away from that damn Messiah: he's everywhere I turn. He's even got me a little agitated about my own eternal destination.'

Johnny started to answer without really thinking: 'It feels . . .' but he had to think: how did it feel? It had happened quickly. The idea. The line. The campaign and now the accolades. In truth, he was surprised by it all and he let this slip. 'It's all a bit sudden,' he said.

'Spare me the humility. I have not brought you to the most expensive restaurant in town to hear how humble you are. Take the credit: Smiling Jesus is your creation.' And Wollard made his tight smile. He was an ugly man but success had given him the confidence of a handsome prince. He was dressed in his wide-shouldered suit, his hair slicked back with precision. He was in his late forties and by far the fittest man at WWW (he had made a science of age deferment) and yet at close quarters, it was apparent that his attire worked a little too hard at arresting nature's inevitable progress.

Wollard fixed Johnny with a highly-charged expression. In his eyes there was the offer of something. Wollard had dished his ration of compliments. He now had another purpose.

'I think that you will benefit greatly from working with a new partner – someone like Bill. I have talked to him about it and he would be delighted to work with you. You can learn a great deal from him. Naturally you will be on a more appropriate salary, something commensurate with the responsibility, but I think you are ready.'

'And Edson?'

Since refusing to work on the LifeGen campaign, Edson's position at WWW had become precarious. Things had looked bad for him ever since Bill, as a joke, had posted Edson's candid and brilliant portrait of Wollard on the Creative Director's door. Admirable though the artistry was, Wollard had chosen to see it as a work of subversion rather than creativity.

'Edson's heart is not in it. He lacks steely ambition, what I like to call the urgency of dedication, and that makes him dead wood. You, however, have an enthusiasm, a desire to do well. I can see that you want success. You are an unevenly yoked pairing, and that could hold you back from achieving what you are capable of achieving.'

Johnny liked Edson, admired him even. Every office needed an Edson to counteract the Wollards of this world and yet WWW was no place for the unambitious. Edson's lack of ambition might, as Wollard was suggesting, hamper Johnny's own prospects of progress. Wollard was offering a golden opportunity: promotion to a position and salary that might take him three or four years to achieve. To show an undue loyalty to his partner now would be foolish.

'I would love to work with Bill,' Johnny said with an ease that surprised him.

'Excellent.'

'What exactly can I expect to be earning?' Johnny asked. It was professional of him to ask this.

'What are you worth?'

Johnny wanted to name a figure that showed he was serious: nothing too ludicrous, nor too modest. A figure that would make a difference to the quality of his life – the flat in Park West Gardens; holidays without compromise; another pair of Grantly Grants.

'Ten thousand more.'

Wollard opened his arms as though the payments were already on their way.

'A car, too,' Johnny said, coolly. He could feel a slight churn in his stomach from the champagne.

'Any one in particular?'

'A Shapiro.'

'GT?'

'Convertible.'

'The Convertible is for director level only. The GT can be arranged.'

'It will be a new challenge,' Johnny said.

'Then you accept?'

'Yes.'

'It's all agreed then. Good. Enough of personnel.'

Johnny pictured Edson floating face down in water with his shirt billowing, then himself, winged and soaring skywards towards a golden sun.

He wondered if he had been coerced into something with a terrible catch to it, a thought that merely flashed through his mind and that he quickly attributed to the perfectly natural flickers of anxiety and unease that accompany unexpected good news.

'Not that it stops there,' Wollard said. 'I want to see more from you. LifeGen want a television commercial and I think we can have some fun with it. I want a brainstorm very soon.'

Johnny's nose was blocked in one nostril and he could feel the tickle of a sneeze buzzing. Wollard grimaced as Johnny caught the explosion in his napkin.

'You'll have no time for colds.'

'It's nothing.'

'I'll tell you a secret,' Wollard said. 'A valuable secret. You must stay fit. In twenty-four years I have never had a day off sick. It's this that has kept me ahead of the race.'

Wollard's heart no doubt pumped perfectly at a cold and callously low pressure, hardened by careful care, like a machine, trained not to feel pain, set to run and run.

'You should join me on one of my morning runs through the park: you look peaky.'

Johnny leant to his left and looked at himself in the gilt-framed rococo mirror behind Wollard. His skin was perhaps a little pale and it contrasted markedly with Wollard's sallow tan. He drank his champagne and imagined himself looking at himself drinking the champagne and wondered whether the quaff was expert enough. Wollard seemed to drink without actually taking any, as though he were keeping a sober advantage: he knew how to enjoy himself today and keep half an eye on tomorrow.

'Let's make a toast,' Wollard said. 'To your future.'

They raised their glasses to his future. The future: a subject treated by life assurance companies and weathermen with confidence, as if it could be measured with an empirical certainty. And yet, outside the predictions of seers, there never had been a foreseeable future. There was no foolproof apparatus to predict it.

Through the chink and sparkle of the cut crystal, Johnny looked for his future and saw instead the splendid interior of the restaurant, distorted and warped. He drank in the crisp liquid and watched the bubbles ascend the crystal flute, burst and disappear.

ELEVEN

Johnny arrived, bleary-eyed and foggy-headed, at the gates of the park, wearing a tracksuit over shorts and shirt, and a bobble hat for extra warmth; his success no longer keeping the cold from getting through to him.

Wollard was already there, jogging on the spot, shooting out controlled breaths of vapour and bringing his hands together in a rhythmic clap that synchronized with his lifting knees. He was dressed to win in the very latest sporting garb.

Johnny energized himself with competitive thoughts.

Come on. Be strong. He's nearly twice your age; don't breathe heavily; don't even let him hear you breathe; set the pace and then force it; don't talk too much; let him do the talking; those clothes won't help him; it'll be him who looks peaky when you've run him off his feet.

Wollard did not pause for idle greeting. He nodded in the direction he wanted to go and set off at a brisk and even pace which immediately stretched Johnny, the leggy yards forcing him to take small quick steps and fast gulps of freezing air which seared his already sore throat.

As Wollard effortlessly galloped he began to talk as though this were a mere amble for him.

'This is the most effective life assurance policy there is,' he said.

Johnny looked down at the bright lines of Wollard's running shoes and in their soft squeaking he thought he heard a jingle:

> *We are fit and*
> *We are strong and*
> *We are go-ing*
> *to live long.*

'There are going to be some changes at the agency: a rationalization,' Wollard continued, without the judder of the run upsetting the delivery of his words.

Johnny tried to focus on the lurid green stripe on Wollard's left foot.

'Come on, young man: knees up: I have a time to beat,' Wollard called. A slight gap was opening up between the two of them now. Johnny's legs were like the legs of another person, someone who had already run twenty miles without sustenance. He wanted to ask Wollard something but he had no breath to spare for talking: even thinking about his breathing seemed to use up valuable oxygen.

'You'll have to pick it up,' Wollard said.

Like a punch-drunk boxer thinking he might yet pull off a sensational knockout, Johnny forced himself to run faster and he caught and overtook Wollard for a few seconds and then flagged again, and then the distance between them lengthened. He had a rasping pain in his throat, a heaving in his chest, dizziness in his head and a stifling temperature. The pulse at his throat beat out an unsteady rhythm:

> *I am slow and*
> *I am weak and*
> *I can hard-ly*
> *ev-en speak.*

Wollard's effortless canter was leeching Johnny's will. His boss was still speaking but Johnny could not keep up to hear what he was saying. Despite the interval between them, Wollard did not, would not, could not slow down;

he was relentless, like a shark that can not stop swimming because if it does it will die.

'You go on,' Johnny said, barely audible to himself.

'I will,' Wollard said and he ran on.

Johnny slumped and bowed to his frailty, curling up in a heaving, disorderly heap. He watched the indestructible Wollard until he became a dot amongst the early-morning walkers. There was something almost supernatural about his boss's fitness, Johnny surmised; perhaps Wollard wasn't really human; perhaps he would not ever die.

Across the park the frost was fading and a million surprising webs spread their silver-thread panoply over the grass, making a city of traps.

The traffic was building up now and humming as it gathered, the city clearing its throat and moving into its own jog, unable to mutiny from its timetabled agenda. Johnny's own body clock, with its automatic propulsions and functions, was complaining and threatening a rebellion and it seemed that with this stuttering Johnny became aware of himself and that an anxiety came creeping into the space that awareness had made.

He didn't like this awareness. It wasn't good to stop and think, he thought. Wollard was proof of that. Self-awareness would kill a man like Wollard. His single-mindedness and emotional detachment were his charter for longevity: he would live long because he never doubted otherwise. And if he had doubts, they were too well disguised to show. Johnny seemed suddenly beset with a nameless fear; like a virus, it had slipped in in his weakness and he cursed himself for being so feeble. How he envied Wollard his blind certainty.

Even a smiling Messiah could not lift Johnny's spirits as he entered the foyer of WWW. To the left of the revolving doors, in the manner of a cinema's 'currently showing' billboards, a board displayed the agency's most recent

70

and germane campaigns. Smiling Jesus was there along-side the stills for Bill Andrews' Connoisseur Cat Food commercial and Wollard's Spreading Oak Building Society – beneath the branches of which customers lived in benign and blissful security.

It was only a poster, and Johnny knew that the gaze of certain portraits could follow you around a room, but as he walked past him and into the building he could feel the eyes of Smiling Jesus at his back.

In the Creative Department there was a great deal of noise and bustle, people were animated and brisk and Johnny's sluggishness contrasted sharply with their staccato, purposeful movements. He marvelled at the natural energy people had, that unthinking puff they possessed.

Taylor was arguing loudly with an executive about a piece of work and Johnny winced at the volume and unnecessary vehemence of it all.

'I don't care if you think the work is too in-your-face. I'm fed up with you guys upstairs brown-nosing the client. We're paid to advise them and this is the work we're going to present. Correction: the work *you're* going to present.' The young man reddened and retreated.

Johnny stared at his desk vacantly, not thinking anything much in particular; then he told himself that he ought to get on with something although he knew not what. He had to think hard about his next move: what was he doing here?

You're here to work.

What work?

The Smiling Jesus commercial ideas.

What about them?

You need to have some for next week's meeting.

Bill Andrews was at his desk already working.

'You look terrible, Yells,' he said. 'You look like a seriously unwell adman who knows that he can't afford to take a day off work in case someone takes his job.'

Johnny was cold from the dried sweat and hot from his flu.

'I need to shower,' Johnny said.

'You might as well move your things over to my desk today,' Bill said, pointing to Edson's empty chair.

'Where is he?' Johnny asked.

'Getting his redundancy cheque. Lucky boy – tax free.'

Johnny had always enjoyed Bill's brashness, it was a trait which flourished in an environment where emotional hardness was a virtue; but now he found it inappropriate and wanting.

'You sound pleased,' Johnny said.

'Don't tell me you're surprised.'

'I can't see what Edson has done to deserve it.'

'W doesn't like him. Anyway, he's won nothing since he's been here.'

No. He just allowed others to pick up awards for him: others, like me, Johnny thought.

Johnny worked up a hypocritical indignation and went up to Personnel to seek out his ex-partner. He found him leaning against the wall outside the office, sequestered in thought.

'This is ridiculous,' Johnny said, not knowing exactly what was ridiculous: the fact that Edson was being fired, the fact that protesting made any difference, or the fact that he was making such a protest when he was partly responsible for Edson's redundancy. Johnny recalled his treacherous silence in the restaurant and the perfidy now whispered at his ear.

You should have said more. You had your chance to defend Edson to Wollard but you kept quiet and now Edson is being sacked. But you don't really care about him. This show of solidarity is a token gesture to appease your own unease.

'I can't believe it,' Johnny said, trying to silence that niggly, internal voice with audible words. He stared at the floor, unable to look Edson in the eye.

'It's in the nature of things,' Edson said.

'But it's . . . so bloody unfair.' Johnny wanted to vent his frustration, he wanted to be angry. How could Edson be so peaceful about it? Where did he get that damn calmness from? It was unhealthy to react so disinterestedly to a dismissal from a good job at the leading advertising agency in the land.

'They're fools. You're better at this than me.'

'Don't run yourself down on my behalf. I'll be fine.'

'But . . . but you were my partner; we've had so many great ideas together.'

'Let's not forget what a great idea is,' Edson said.

Johnny wanted to somehow justify himself, to justify what he still did. 'What did Wollard say?'

'He said, "I am afraid that we are going to have to lose you".'

Johnny could well imagine the scene: a smiling Wollard making a little speech about the need to cut back, falling profits, the loss of a client or two; then a token compliment about a useful contribution quickly balanced by some specific personal criticism – a lack of ambition, not quite fitting in – which would have the ring of half truth to it and which Edson would not disagree with. All the time Wollard would be smiling a resigned smile and playing the reluctant firer (even a man like Wollard wanted to be remembered in a favourable light, to retain the patina of popularity). He'd then add that it was nothing personal (the portrait would not be part of the discussion) whilst offering some telephone numbers for freelance work, and a final, consolation shake of his cool, glabrous hand. And so, still smiling sympathetically, the big fish would swallow the little fish.

'It's all so bloody cut-throat,' Johnny went on.

'The trick there is to keep your chin down, pressed firmly against your chest,' Edson said.

As he said this Edson looked at Johnny as though he knew what Johnny was thinking and what he had done. Edson was looking straight at and into him and Johnny could not meet his gaze. Was it an innocent clairvoyance, or was Edson deliberately probing him? Johnny felt like a pane of glass behind which his darker thoughts could all be seen bubbling and troubling.

'I wish you wouldn't look at me like that,' he said. 'As though you feel sorry for me or something, as though I'm the one who's been sacked.'

'You don't look great, Johnny. You look tired and edgy.'

'Damn right, I'm edgy. It could be me next.'

'Not if Wollard has anything to do with it. He has his eye on you. I think he's grooming a successor.'

A door in Personnel opened and, with her well-practised sympathetic face, the Personnel Officer asked Edson in.

Johnny wanted to offer Edson something more supportive than a handshake: bosses offered handshakes, even when they fired you, but he could not bring himself to offer anything more than that. 'Don't lose touch,' Edson said, holding on to Johnny's hand longer than Johnny wanted. Johnny blushed. He actually felt close to tears but he convinced himself that it was the flu that was making his eyes water and nothing else.

As he walked back to the ground floor, he kept his head bowed and his hands about his eyes and nose for fear that someone might see. In the corridor he passed Taylor who asked him if he was all right.

'I'm fine,' Johnny lied. Not saying what you meant came easily at work; it was part of the language of survival, part of the staying ahead.

TWELVE

Even before opening his eyes, Johnny could tell that it was late and that the day was well into taking care of itself without him. He could hear traffic on the road outside, the sounds of a neighbour pottering in the garden and the sonorous buzz of voices on the clock radio that had failed to wake him. The light that seeped through the small gap in the curtain created a half light that made things crepuscular and ill-defined. Penny's side of the bed was cool and the duvet there had been pulled up over the pillow which had long lost the heat and the imprint from her head.

In the last few days his limbs had become heavy and his head light and thick – symptoms which corresponded to those of the flu as outlined in the newspaper: heavy legs, a dull ache throughout the muscles, light-sensitive headaches and a vague, listless feeling. He could feel it in his legs and he rubbed the back of his thighs where the deep ache lay.

Johnny rolled over. He felt bruised and disorientated by this new and capricious sleeping pattern. It was noon and he had lost any sense of it being a particular day. He felt sweat at his back, trickling from his armpits, actually trickling as though he had been running. It didn't seem possible that he would shrug off this malaise, it seemed to him now that he had always felt this way.

As he lay there, strangely torpid, he felt his mind separate into a kind of argument

What are you doing in bed?

I am not feeling well.

You are not really that ill.

I feel terrible. I ache all over.

It's an excuse, a deferment of responsibility. You should be at work.

I'm going to the doctor.

I'm going to dock your pay.

I want to do well. I want to be well.

You are well. You don't have flu: you're not even sniffing. It's all in your mind.

You are my mind, don't forget that. You – that voice that I am talking to – that is my voice, so don't try to tell me what to do. Now leave me. I must sleep. I am weary.

You are tiresome.

I am tired.

We are all getting very tired of you.

Please let me sleep. Give me some peace.

A piece of my mind.

Stop punning.

No. You're the pun-merchant; that's what you do. That's all you do: construct feeble double meanings from words.

Let me sleep.

Sheep, sheep, sheep, sheep.

But sleep wouldn't come; his schismatic mind continued to pick an argument and Johnny could not silence it. The voices were both his, one a slandering, malicious little voice, that had the tone of a reasonable doctor and then a hectoring parent; the other weak but somehow more truly the sound of himself.

When he thought he was clearing a blank space in his head, the argument began to subvert his peace.

Don't you think you should get up now? Don't you think you should go to work? You've already missed two days. You've got the commercial ideas to come up with. You'll be fired next if you're not careful. Think of that. You're about to buy your first home with your well-earned and recently raised salary

76

and you're throwing it away because you can not be bothered to get out of bed.

Smiling Jesus looked down from the wall. Johnny had stuck up a LifeGen poster above his bed as a memento of his success; it was like a swimming certificate or a diploma, it possessed a certain reassurance, a confirmation of things achieved. Johnny would for ever be able to call upon the name of Smiling Jesus as proof of his ability.

Johnny knew that if someone stared at a picture long enough they might start to see it differently; that it was even possible for a picture to seem to absorb the thoughts and impressions and mood of the viewer to such an extent that it began to reflect their state of mind. Perhaps that explained why the face looked a little different to him now.

Don't look at me like that. Remember that I was the one that saw you cowering and lost in the corner of that cracked and dank building you'd been living in for all those years. It was me that put the smile back on your face, so you can damn well smile at me now.

But the face in the poster did not respond to his command. It continued to look at him with what seemed a kind of pity, rather than any condemnation. He looked away not believing it and he swung his legs as athletically as he could to the floor and stood and stretched away the pain and galvanized himself with thoughts of work and food and getting on with life.

'I'll have breakfast,' he said, out loud, and he took himself downstairs, temporarily forgetting his aches and pains and the transmogrifying poster.

He spurned life-enhancing oats, semi-skimmed milk and banana, and instead gathered everything that it was possible to fry: eggs, bacon, sausages, mushrooms, bread, tomatoes. He melted some full-fat butter until it scintillated and then he tossed the food into the pan.

'Starve a fever; feed a cold,' he said.

As the food fried pell-mell, he brewed up a pot of coffee and made toast and to stop himself thinking he picked up a newspaper from a week ago and read a story about a man who was sailing around the world with his dog, a review of a film that he must see and an encouraging piece about property prices being at their lowest point in six months.

There was a message on the answer machine, from Judy at work:

'Johnny? Are you there? Hope you're feeling better. W wanted me to see if you can make the LifeGen brainstorm. For the meeting Monday. He's concerned to keep things moving. Give me a call.'

Johnny pictured the scene at work: people bustling about with justified self-importance, Wollard overseeing the regime, everything working well enough without him. What advantage had he lost in these last three days? Even with his recent success he was dispensable.

Relax. Everyone is ill sometimes.

Except Wollard.

The doctors' waiting room was full of people coughing and sniffing. It resembled a crowded airport in a war-torn country where the refugees were desperately trying to get the next plane back to Healthland.

Healthland had its own borders, currency and citizens; it was a place where everyone wanted to live and many did live, not realizing they lived there until they were deprived of its freedoms. Some of these people would soon enough be granted their visas, their bill of health. Others might wait in transit for longer than they bargained for whilst their bodies went though the bureaucracy of recovery.

Healthland; Sickland.

Johnny looked at the people and tried to guess which country they were destined for. Next to him, against the adjacent wall, an elderly man leaned forward and coughed a percolating liquid cough at the floor. His face was sunken and grey and he blinked very slowly. He looked sideways and raised his eyebrows at Johnny as if to say he blamed no-one but himself for his malaise. His yellowed fingertips and the broken, distempered skin about his nose showed that he was a smoker and a drinker. He was never going to get back to Healthland. Not even the asylum of medicine would get him there. Was there a suggestion in the man's look that they were all in the same boat here, all ill and in simple need of medicine?

Not on your life.

Johnny looked away from the man, wanting to have nothing to do with him.

His destination is not mine: I am young and he is old; he has a serious, self-inflicted illness, I have a random flu bug. He has taken up permanent residence in Sickland, I will soon be taking my place back in the blooming air of Healthland.

Johnny picked up a magazine from the table. It was several months out of date but its colourful transience was reassuring to him; everyone in the magazine was very well indeed: healthy complexions, muscle definition perfect. This was Healthland's brochure and these people its choice representatives. No bad teeth, no spots, no smokers' fingers: nothing rebarbative whatsoever.

A nurse entered the room and called out a name: 'Mr Burton?' The man with the sunken face raised himself with difficulty and moved along the corridor like a phantom.

Look at him: he's resigned to it. It is a question of attitude. If you think you will be well, then you will be well. You must show this attitude to the doctor. Doctors like good attitude. Good attitude is more effective than a course of antibiotics.

His doctor was a young woman who looked tired but sympathetic. 'What can I do for you?' she asked. From her tone she must have been surprised to see a healthy young man standing before her, Johnny thought, and he almost wanted to say that he was fine and that he shouldn't be here at all.

'I think I've got this flu,' he said. 'I've been feeling a bit achy for a few days and my head hurts. I'll probably shake it off but I need to get back to work.'

'Let's have a look at you; can you take your shirt off?' the doctor asked.

'Sure,' Johnny said, wanting to play everything down and show that his ability to co-operate was a sure sign of well being. She listened to his chest and then looked into his throat which he gladly opened wide for her inspection. After that he said that he needed a sick note for the three days that he'd missed.

'Let me take your blood pressure,' the doctor said and Johnny wondered if she had found something and wasn't telling him. He prattled nervously as she placed the rubber pump bag about his arm and inflated it until it hurt his bicep.

'Is this flu actually from another country?' he asked.

'There are many variants.'

'Can you give me something for it: a jab, antibiotics or something?'

'We'll see. Hold still, please.' She let the air depress and scribbled a figure in her notes.

'Normal?' Johnny asked.

'Fine.'

'Is it good?'

'It's normal.'

'Is that good?'

'Normal is good.'

'My heart okay?'

'It sounds fine.'

'Would you be able to tell if it wasn't, just by listening?'

'If I thought there was something wrong I would get it scanned.'

'This is a bad time for me to be sick.'

'There's never a good time to be sick. What line of work are you in?'

'Advertising. I'm a copywriter. I write headlines and jingles.'

'Have you done anything I might have seen on the telly?'

'We do the Connoisseur Cat Food campaign.'

The doctor gave a smile of recognition. 'The one with the aristocratic cat? I love that, although I must confess I give my cat Bisky Bites.' The doctor quoted the line: ' "Nine lives simply isn't enough for a cat like me." Did you do that?'

'Yes. Well, it wasn't actually my ad.'

Johnny thought he'd tell Bill Andrews that his advertisement had failed to make his doctor change her cat food from Bisky Bites to Connoisseur. It was one thing to like an advertisement, another to actually respond to it. He would definitely mention this to Bill when he next saw him.

'It must be quite stressful having to come up with ideas all the time.'

'No more stressful than being a doctor,' Johnny replied.

'You can put your shirt back on. You must have a good imagination for those things,' she said.

Johnny said he hoped he did.

'I'll give you something for the aches and pains and a sick note for the days you've missed. You'll be back to normal in a few days.'

Normal. Johnny pictured himself as normal and saw his old self laughing and getting on with the business of life without cares or worries. Normal was not realizing that you were normal. It was an innocent, some would say ignorant, state of existence. He wanted to be normal again, for the doctor to give him a slip of paper, perhaps a plaque, saying 'normal'.

Afterwards he wondered if he should have mentioned

his insomnia, the dreams, the discourse between the two voices in his head, his mounting fear of death, the fact that he did not feel entirely 'himself', and the changing face, but none of these 'symptoms' were clinical enough. And anyway, the doctor wouldn't have taken long to explain them, she'd not need a special instrument to locate their source, a stethoscope to press against some inner part of him and detect the origin of the problem; she'd simply tell him that he was a little stressed and that such things were the consequence of having a lively imagination.

THIRTEEN

Johnny decided to talk to Albert. It was too dangerous to share his fears with anyone at work, and Penny would only worry about him. He needed someone neutral, someone sane, someone he could trust. A good friend was better medicine than a doctor and an hour spent in their company a week's therapy. Albert was intelligent and wise; Johnny could count on Albert for considered opinions and advice. Albert was not given to persiflage and never answered unless he was certain of a thing. He was sceptical but his scepticism was not cynical; it was a requirement expedient of his profession: things had to be proven before a statement could be made. He was not loquacious; when he did speak his words were as measured and meaningful as one of his dark, courtroom suits. His judgements were based on the solid foundations of a fine intellect and implacable reason. He would allay Johnny's creeping anxieties. He would put Johnny's fears in the dock and sentence them away.

It was a Friday night and the two friends went to the Fox and the Grapes. It was reassuring to go to the pub, Johnny felt: the pub was earthy and lively and would be full of people seemingly without cares. As they walked, Johnny tried to convince himself of his good health and hush the hurly-burly in his head.

'I've got some catching up to do: no beer for a week now,' he said.

'How are you feeling?' Albert asked.

'Better. Much better.'

At the pub, Johnny saw the painted sign above the saloon door depicting a slitty-eyed fox looking up longingly at the grapes. Inside, the pub was packed full of people who were still reaching for the grapes, straining for the fruit and some who had already grabbed it. There were no free chairs and so the two young men made their way to a break in the bar and leant against it. The lively sounds and esculent smells reminded Johnny that life was thrilling and sensuous and that he had been getting far too much into his own head of late. It was not healthy to think too much, it was better to enjoy and just be.

Albert looked well and handsome in his suit. His jet hair and olive clear skin gave him an exotic air. Handsome, intelligent and successful: what a combination, Johnny thought.

Albert bought the beers and although Johnny feared the prospect of a full pint he could not ask for a half. He wanted to authenticate his normality by having the full measure that a normal healthy young man is expected to drink.

'To your good health,' Albert said.

'Yes,' Johnny said and he took a tentative sip. 'How was your trip?'

'Grizzly.'

Johnny wanted to hear the details; it would help him to forget himself.

'Tell me about it.'

Albert took a slow and long gulp from his beer, almost drinking half the pint already. Johnny took another sip from his own.

'A stabbing on a train. The man is pleading insanity.'

'Is he guilty?'

'Yes. But his state of mind will affect the sentence.'

Albert began to explain the case in greater detail. Johnny found it hard to concentrate on the finer points of the story and his mind drifted back to his own fear.

The noise was pressing in on him and he was struggling to hear Albert. The music of conversation was so loud and antiphonal that Johnny wondered how anyone could hear what they were saying. 'Do you think we could sit down on the floor there?' he asked.

They made their way to the bit of floor where there were some pipes thick enough to sit on. Standing in a circle in front of the pipes a quartet of men each held their pint glasses nonchalantly in one hand and amused each other with banter which every now and again raised an uproarious, joyless laugh from all of them.

What are they laughing about? Johnny wondered. Why are they in such great good humour? He knew well enough: they had no fear. Their youth, the beer's dulling effect, the proximity of company, the throb of life were all enough to convince them that there was nothing to fear, that they were perhaps immortal. That was what immortality was: not being afraid. A man could reach the age of twenty-nine without once contemplating his own end; but now 'the end' seemed to be presenting itself to him in every little thing he saw.

He felt afraid again. People could drink a lot and they could stand and talk without need of a chair; they were young and not afraid of death; they could talk without pausing for breath; they weren't worried about life assurance or what happened when they died. Perhaps Albert feared these things too and covered them more effectively; Johnny guessed, from his friend's calm assurance, that he had some airtight philosophy all worked out. 'What do you think happens when we die?' Johnny asked, trying to make the question sound casual.

'Why do you ask?'

'I'm just curious.'

Albert did not deliberate over his reply; it was like a fact, readily to hand.

'It will be as we were before we were born: nothing.' Albert had the knack of making everything he said sound

85

gospel. Johnny pictured nothing for ever and felt its cold plausibility.

The 'immortals' in the circle broke out into a particularly abrasive laugh as though the whole joke were on every person in the pub and only they had got the punch line.

'What if there is something after death?'

'You're not getting religion are you, Johnny? You're getting that look – a little pale and cadaverous.'

Johnny had no thought for religion but he wanted to say that he was afraid of death. He was afraid of death and he was afraid of his fear of death. But here was Albert who had no illusions, no straw-clutching fantasies and a perfect calm in predicting total annihilation. Was he genuinely unafraid or expertly covering up, a barrister eloquently defending a weak position?

'Aren't you a little afraid?' Johnny persisted.

Albert seemed slightly irritated and Johnny wondered if his questions were stupid ones. No doubt Albert was above this callow line of thought. He had probably discussed these issues and made his conclusions as a thirteen-year-old whilst smoking behind bike sheds at school.

'What's to be afraid of? You can't fear what can not be known. Stick to what you do know. Enjoy what you have. This is our one life.'

He is right. Listen to the voice of reason. This is your one life.

Albert asked Johnny if he wanted another beer and Johnny accepted, being as natural as he possibly could about it and cupping what was left of his first pint to hide the fact that he had barely drunk half. What he had drunk was fermenting with a triple strength inside him and making him heady.

The two friends found easier, less uncertain ground to cover: films they wanted to see, books they had read. And of course there was the fact that Johnny and Penny's offer on 29 Clamber Road had finally been accepted: they expected to be in in two months' time, once they had secured a mortgage. Johnny thanked Albert for his generously low rent and for allowing him the run of the place in his frequent absences. It was better talking about these practical and mundane realities than speculating over the unknowable.

When Johnny got up to go to the toilet Albert pointed to his half-drunk glass.

'Are you going to drink that?'

'Yes, of course,' Johnny said. 'I'm just going to the toilet.'

He went, and took his pint with him, asking himself why he couldn't just admit to Albert that he didn't feel up to finishing his beer. At the basin he looked into the mirror and saw that he was a little pale and thin. Dark circles gathered around his eyes.

Look where your philosophizing is taking you. You look terrible.

He still had three quarters of a pint left in his glass and he held it to his chest while urinating. He waited until he was alone and then poured the liquid into the bowl. As he re-entered the bar he held the lip of the glass at his mouth and when he could see Albert he made the pretence of knocking back the final dregs.

Later, walking home, Johnny felt his feet on the ground and that vague pull of gravity pressing him to the earth which turned beneath the bright cold canopy above. This was where he was and he must lay his foundations here on the earth and get from it what he could while he was here. People like Albert and Wollard and Penny were successful and content because they knew their place in the scheme of things. They had no illusions or cod beliefs. They were rooted in the here, the now, the seen and the felt, trusting in the reality of this life now, not some other next life. Only fools believed such things.

'Perhaps you should have some of this,' Albert said, licking the paper for his illicit smoke. 'It can bring on moments of great calm and clarity. I often have one before a tricky case.'

Johnny watched Albert roll the joint, sitting on the wall of the back garden. The lawyer was as meticulous and sure with the drug as he was with a nasty bit of tort. Albert stroked and smoothed the roll and tapped its open ends. He lit it, inhaled it deeply and blew out the smoke in a steady puff.

'Manna,' he said.

He took another and passed it to Johnny who inhaled with a degree of desperation, sucking hard and closing his eyes. He saw the little sparks of light in his head and felt his breathing change.

The two of them became quiet for the rest of the night, enjoying the peace while it lasted. Even stoned, Albert retained his clear-headed, balanced calm.

Later that night, lying on his bed, Johnny spun up and away from the solid ground. When he did fall asleep he dreamt a dream that did not give itself away as a dream until he woke.

He dreamt that he was at a trial. The courtroom was packed and everyone was wearing barristers' wigs. It soon became apparent that it was his own trial, that he was the one being prosecuted, and that the jury was made up of everyone present: a number far in excess of the mandatory twelve. These people – a hundred of them – were frowning. They were all looking at him as if he were already guilty. Some of them were drinking, which surely was not allowed, even in a dreamed-up court.

'They're all drinking, Your Honour,' Johnny whimpered at the judge; but the judge waved him away and took a swig from a gallon flagon, letting the slops run down the side of his face, wet his whiskers and spoil the silk of his gown.

Johnny was led to the dock where the charges against him were read out very loudly by a man with a grating, high-pitched voice that everyone, even the cavorting drunkards in the top gallery, could hear except for Johnny. He couldn't deny the charges because he didn't know what they were.

The judge smiled and wiped his mouth on his sleeve and banged his gavel upon the bench. There was an awed, respectful silence as the sentence was read:

'I sentence you to nothing for ever, young man.'

'Nothing where?'

'Why, you fool, nothing nowhere. Nothing for ever-more. Nothing for always and on and on and on for ever, ad infinitum, in perpetuity, everlasting, continuous, non-stop, unending nothing! Take him away.'

And Johnny was taken away in complete silence and led to a cell which was black, so black that he could not work out whether its walls were five or five thousand feet apart; and then, although he could not see, he felt the darkness close in around him and the darkness of the cell was as nothing compared to the new, dark dark-ness that was all around him and he was scared and the darkness seemed to envelop him although not quite because he was aware of himself and he thought that he must hold on to the self because that's where his life was. But then it seemed to slip from him, this idea of himself, until he couldn't remember himself; he was for-gotten like a textbook fact from his youth. And then the darkness became grey and there were shapes and he became conscious of objects he recognized, and crossing the divide between sleep and wakefulness he saw his bed, the lampshade, the mirror and the poster of the once-Smiling Jesus.

FOURTEEN

At WWW a brainstorm was conducted with strict observance. The 'storming' room was sparse, always containing exactly eight chairs, a long, oblong glass table and a flip-chart. The cold, ascetic atmosphere was probably meant to reflect the clearing of clutter needed for ideas to move about freely. And, to facilitate the flow of ideas, a pot of coffee and a plate of biscuits were placed in the middle of the table: a biscuit each; a coffee each. The coffee was poured, the biscuits broken, then there followed a moment's silence and reflection before the ideas came and filled the room with light. Every utterance, however obscure or banal, was written and recorded by a chairperson.

Richards, the LifeGen account man, was chairperson for the day. He stood by the flip-chart and a cardboard cutout of Smiling Jesus which lay propped against the wall, looking with benevolence upon all the admen, except for Johnny who saw something admonishing in the Messiah's cold, cardboard stare. He felt that if Smiling Jesus had walked in today, he would have strode into the agency, passed the fig tree, blessed the receptionists, healed someone with a headache, and then entered the boardroom and offered them all eternal life, except him.

Are you mad? Pull yourself together.

Johnny had missed a few days' work and already things had moved on without him; he must impose himself. He forced himself to look attentive; he set his features into a look of calm authority and listened to Richards get things underway.

'To get you up to speed, Johnny. The client loves your friend here. He's their saviour, and ours. The image is already part of the fabric. Recognition is superb. The poster ads had the highest recall of any campaign last month. We don't have accurate response figures yet, but the signs are good. Research shows that the campaign was successful because: one, it caught the eye; two, it made people think about life assurance; and three, the punters liked him, with his friendly reassuring smile. He makes them feel comfortable. Our initial concerns that some people might be offended have not been borne out. Apart from the bishop, Standards have had no complaints. It seems we can do what we like with Smiling Jesus.

'We have the budget for two thirty-second commercials, or a one-minuter if we prefer. They can be linked if LifeGen want us to pick up on and develop the life after death theme. And they want us to be bold. I think we have an opportunity here to slam something so hard into the minds of the punters that they will not be able to get up in the morning without thinking "I must talk to LifeGen".'

Highest recall. Big budget. His creation praised. This should have been sweet music to Johnny, but the statistics seemed to accuse him, like the changed expression of the cardboard creation there at the end of the room.

'So. Let's pour the coffee and see what happens.'

The executive flipped the chart and pulled the top from his black marker pen.

Johnny tried to clear a space in his own mind, to put aside earthly things: the still nagging question of buying his house, the odd turn of his mind. Bill, who could not hide his need to impress Wollard whenever he could, opened.

'I think we need to get a little more aggressive – tap

into that millennial fear people are feeling. The posters were friendly, they got people to take notice. Now we need to scare them. Give them hell.'

The executive wrote hell, millennial and aggressive.

'And what does hell conjure up for you?' Richards asked, oiling the proceedings.

Familiar hellish clichés began to flow from the mouths of the gathering.

'Screaming.'

'Pain. Eternal agony.'

'Fire.'

'The Devil.'

Richards wrote them all down.

'Hell could be a place where people go when they don't have LifeGen life assurance.'

'Exactly,' Wollard said.

'People tumbling into an inferno and saying: "If only we'd talked to LifeGen," Bill went on. 'That's it. Hell is where people who haven't talked to LifeGen are going to end up. The punters arrive at the gates of heaven. St Peter asks them if they've taken out a policy with LifeGen. They start to tremble as he looks at his checkboard and sees that they're not on his list. When they realize that they're not down they start to wail and gnash their teeth. Then they start their descent.'

'Is it me or is anyone else hot?' Johnny asked.

'It's you,' Bill said.

'So should we have a heaven?' Taylor put in.

Richards wrote 'heaven'.

'A place where good and faithful LifeGen policyholders go. A place where people are eternally thankful that they talked to LifeGen,' Bill said, very excited now. 'Yeah, in heaven they enjoy the eternal benefits of LifeGen's policies.'

'Lovely,' Wollard said. 'The Devil himself could not have done better.'

Johnny pictured hell and saw a cave receding to a

pin-sized hole; the walls of the cave were pink and fleshy and a river flowed through its middle; the cave was a mouth and the river was a tongue flowing down the gullet; the mouth was screaming and the tongue flowed with words that came straight from hell's maw.

He tried to picture heaven and he couldn't focus on an image of it.

He slipped from the vision to reality and saw that he had contributed nothing towards the fast-extending list. He had not had any clear ideas for the commercial and his ability to concentrate was hampered by an ache at the back of his head near the top of his spine that felt like a bubble. He looked at Wollard and at Bill Andrews and tried to think of something intelligent and authoritative to say.

'This is all fun, but should we be frightening people?' he asked.

'For every fear there is a product,' Wollard said, reciting his favourite maxim.

Hell followed Johnny from the workplace and sat whispering fear to him as he had his end-of-week drink with Bill, Taylor and other staff from the agency. It was a ritual he had once performed with zeal, but he had lost his faith, and he sat there, a troubled, forlorn figure, drinking fruit juice.

Bill was off describing his hell again. Bill's hell was a familiar, bearable hell. In Bill's hell you did at least exist; you were there to smell the sulphur and hear the screams. But Johnny was thinking about it and he didn't believe in Bill's hell. Whatever hell lay beyond this life he guessed to be far worse than anything man could dream up. Hell was a cold, cold nothing, a nothing that he could not hold in his head for more than a second without wishing for the hot eternal damnation Bill foresaw. Hell was a limbo, an almost nearly not-quiteness, an opportunity close to grasping but not taken. Hell was an awareness of mistakes made, wrong turnings taken and no chance of ever rectifying these things.

'We need a devil,' Bill said. 'We need someone to play the Devil. And to my mind, there's only one candidate.' He was getting drunk fast and his lazy eye was drooping.

Johnny felt witless and supine. He shrugged, unable to imagine a suitable candidate. 'I don't know.'

' "For every fear there's a product," ha! ha! ha!'

Johnny could see it.

'Jesus is a little trickier,' Bill said. He paused to let Johnny try and cast Jesus.

Johnny shook his head.

'Edson?' Taylor suggested. Bill began to laugh.

'Nah. That would be against his religion,' he said. 'Come on Yells, you're drinking like a girl.'

When Bill started to become maudlin and cross-eyed and too drunk to be offended, Johnny slipped away, to get home to bed, to get away from the thoughts in his head.

If there's a hell, it's cold, he thought as he leant against the rubber armrest of the escalator that took him down to the underground station. He absently observed the advertisements that descended with him. A theatre show. An insurance company. A novel. So much to see, so much to do. In hell there would be nothing to do. For ever.

Down, down under the city went the steel stairs. At the bottom he felt a warm breeze, wafting up from the earth's hot centre, through some deep connecting shaft.

Hell doesn't exist. And there is no heaven. There's just nothing – and that is worse.

On the platform he could hear the screams of trains bulleting through the black labyrinth. In this city it was possible to get from one place to another without ever stepping into natural light.

On the train, he was struck by the fact that he was not himself again. His fear was now manifesting itself physically: he was conscious of his breathing, the pulse in his neck, his sweaty palms and a fluttering stomach. That great nothing he had pictured for a moment had undone him; but then a man couldn't comprehend the infinite for too long without feeling dizzy. He thought that he might not make it home and he fought off this thought by reading the paper which utterly failed to console or distract him. He stared at the page as though it were a mirror; his eyes were not picking up the words; they were turned inward upon himself.

Next to him, a woman was reading a book and he envied her enjoyment, her ability to escape herself. His mind was finding it increasingly difficult to focus on anything outside himself. He put the paper aside and tried to read the advertisements in the strips but his eyes hurt and the shaking train was making his head ache. Everything seemed too loud, too bright and too vivid.

'Are you all right, young man?'

An elderly woman at his right addressed him, leaning in to look at his face. Johnny was embarrassed to be asked this. The woman reading the book was looking at him, too, the way someone looks at a desperate person.

'I'm fine, thanks,' he said. It alarmed him that a complete stranger should ask him if he was all right. Was it that obvious, that glaring, that he wasn't? He closed his eyes and pretended to sleep, trying to shut out his phobias, but the apprehension was already inside him; he couldn't shut it out by closing his eyes. So he looked out into the rushing black for the sparks of light that sometimes flashed up from the train, wondering why that woman thought he wasn't all right and afraid of what her answer might be.

FIFTEEN

Johnny woke with the jolt of coming out of half-dreams. The pleasure that comes from short journey naps passed with the realization that he had overslept his stop and come to the end of the line.

Downs! *Christ*! *What is wrong with you*?

Some key part of him wasn't functioning; the part that kept the unthinking cogs of his life turning.

According to the station clock it was eleven thirty. The train was clearly going no further. The lights in the carriage were dimmed on half power and there was a phantom quiet. It was black and strange outside as he walked to the ticket office where there was a guard looking up.

'Could you tell me when the next train back to Morton Road is?' Johnny asked.

'Five,' the guard said, without looking up.

'You're joking.'

'Not at this time of night, I'm not.'

Johnny looked back along the platform towards his overshot destination, hardly believing it. He walked to the taxi rank but there were no taxis. The guard told him that he should call a cab from the public telephone box at the end of the road.

Pushing his hands into his pockets and fearful of the lamplit quiet, Johnny whistled his way to the phone box, keeping the whistle low enough not to draw attention his way but loud enough to quell the jitters that were vibrating inside him.

The receiver dangled from the box as if someone had been assailed in mid-conversation. The coin slot was jammed with a bent coin. It was a common enough occurrence, but to Johnny this was no arbitrary piece of vandalism; it was a considered act timed for this moment now, for him here.

He walked on in search of a working booth or perhaps a passing taxi – a forlorn hope in this part of the city. He was in Downs, an undesirable stretch of terraced housing and forgotten industrial buildings. Taxis would not be loitering for custom here. The houses were dark and close and he looked around suspiciously, hearing in the wake of his own footsteps a speedy echo. He tried to dull the conspicuous, strident clicking of his shoes by walking on his toes.

He came to a bus shelter but the timetable was defaced. *If there is a hell it will be like this. A place where you least want to be at a time you least want to be there, separated from all things that you want.*

He gnashed his teeth at the thought of the warm bed he was not in, the brushed-cotton sheets cocooning him, and Penny's welcome curve. There was some unseen power working against him, some invisible, malign conspiracy. The luck that had turned things in his favour was flipping over. Why not? If a coin could land on tails, the same side up, five times in a row, then it would eventually land as heads. Things could change. A man who believes in the randomness of life must surely accept the vagaries of chance without complaint.

A car passed and he put out his arm thinking that it was a taxi, but as it drove past someone in the back of the car jeered at him, the insult exposing him like a searchlight.

'Wankaaaar . . .'

It was a fair description, he felt, as the car sped away to its snug, smug destination.

He stopped walking and considered returning to the

station. Maybe he could get the guard to call a cab if he was still there. The threat of the darkness seemed to make an hour of the minutes. The utter pointlessness of being here made him want to stamp his feet and scream.

Perhaps you were meant to miss your stop. Perhaps if you had got off at the right station you'd have walked home and crossed the road at precisely the point when a police car was passing at high speed and been killed.

Don't delude yourself. You could construct as many elaborate maybes as you like but there is no hidden meaning in this back-to-back stacking of avoidable events. You're here because you missed the stop; you missed the stop because you are tired; you are tired because you have been sleeping badly; you have been sleeping badly because you are anxious; you are anxious because you missed a few days' work.

As he stood there mulling the reasons for being here he realized that Edson lived in Downs. He pulled his life organizer from his bag. Edson. Elderberry Avenue. 43? It looked like 43, but it could have been 48.

It's too late to see him. He'll be asleep. His place could be miles away.

Go and see him. You can get a cab from there.

It is this wracked dithering that's got you here, not some meaningful benign power. It's late. It's not fate.

Go and see Edson.

The voices argued on and he heeded the gently insistent one.

Yes, it was late. Yes, he was tired and yes he could find another phone, but.

Surely you're not considering looking for his house, at eleven o'clock at night?

Johnny could not make the decision based on anything rational, so he let something irrational make it for him.

If I find his street in the next ten minutes, I'll see if he's in.

You could develop a real talent for looking for meaning in meaningless things if you're not careful. You'll be telling me

98

that the name of that road there has a revelatory instruction buried within it.

'Enderby Road.'

E for Edson. End for the End of the line. End by the road. He was good at the game and the connections came thick and fast if he looked hard enough. A shadowy figure clicked along the pavement towards him.

Now look what you've got yourself into. A murderer; a copy-writer and nobody here to witness a thing.

He clenched his fists in his coat and prepared to engage the man, planning in his head the leap and then the clasping of the attacker's head in his hands and the pull-ing of his head onto his knee to the sound of the man's nose cracking like balsa.

I should have got the guard to call a cab.

Indeed, you should.

'Lookin' for somewhere to go, mister?' the man said, slurred, but friendly.

'Elderberry Avenue,' Johnny said, loud and clear. Per-haps if he talked loud enough there would be witnesses. 'Is it near?'

The man's movements were exaggerated by his inebri-ation and he took his time.

'Just over the bridge. Keep going, going, keep going, all the way to the end of the street and it's at the end there. On the left, I think.' How many wrong turnings lay in that 'I think', Johnny wondered.

'How long will it take me?'

'About ten minutes,' the man said.

This tightrope walk between point and pointlessness was a delicate thing, a chancy affair in itself. But there was his answer.

I can't believe you're doing this. You'd base your next steps on the sotted mumblings of a complete stranger. And you don't even know the number. What if it's 48?

Maybe his name will be written by the bell.

Johnny walked on, ignoring the supposed voice of

reason, heeding the other voice – the gentler one – egging him on to Edson. And it occurred to him that maybe Edson might (it was embarrassing, he knew) shed some light on his recent strange turn; Edson who believed in 'all that stuff'.

He strode with purpose.

At the end of the long road he came to Elderberry Avenue. It was not a street he'd choose to live in and the houses made him glad that he lived where he did, but he was warmed at the sight of the lights on in some of them. The doubting, eminently sensible voice sounded off again.

What are you going to do? Knock on 43 and 48? Even if you get the right one and he's in, what then? Are you going to walk in and say, hey, Eddy, I've been having bad dreams and I've got this voice and I think the face in the poster is changing its expression. Oh, and while I'm here, I might as well say that I did nothing to stop Wollard getting rid of you.

Both 43 and 48 had lights on, upstairs. He stood in the dark and it seemed he hovered there for hours.

If you stand here much longer you'll be reported on suspicion of burglary. Go home. It's too late now.

A yellowy mist was creeping at the pavement, the little tongues of vapour licking at his boots. A light went off in one of the bedroom windows. Just then a car cruised slowly towards him and he saw the light of its meter.

Taxi! Thank God.

Without thinking he raised his hand; the cab slowed and growled as he got in.

'Can you get me to Morton Road?' he asked.

'You were lucky,' the cab driver said. 'I was just about to pack it in for the night and go home myself.'

Inside the taxi Johnny was shaking; his heart pattering from the missed encounter. To calm himself Johnny read the advertisement displayed in the taxi cabin's two panels, over and over again.

'Stressed? Call our 24-hour Stressline 0800 500500

and book an appointment at the Crystal Waters Health Centre.'

If you're looking for a sign there it is. Advertising at its best: timely and appropriate: speaking to the need of the individual: think of the tired, pressured people that have slumped into the back of this cab late at night and felt comforted by those words. You should go. 0800 500500. That's an easy number to remember.

And as the taxi sped him home, Johnny memorized the number. At least it might help him take his mind off death for a day.

SIXTEEN

The Golden Plaque Awards ceremony took place in the Great Hall of the Halcyon Vista Hotel, a venue capable of seating one thousand guests. WWW were well represented and, this year, their esteemed and respected Creative Director had been asked to speak to the gathering.

At Table Twenty, Johnny sat with Penny, Bill Andrews and his girlfriend, Taylor and his wife, Wollard and a beautiful woman whom Johnny presumed to be Wollard's girlfriend. The table had been thoughtfully decorated with miniature replica Golden Plaques holding the name of each guest so that everyone might share in the sense of creative success for the evening.

The real plaques were on a Perspex table on stage and the light had been angled to get the maximum sparkle from them. Johnny had seen them the moment he'd entered the glittery hall. They were simple in design: a triangular solid on a stem, like a miniature, golden Christmas tree.

Johnny looked through the programme at the nominations for this year's awards. He was nervous. A Golden Plaque would seal his position at the agency at a time when he needed it. It would give him a kind of irreproachability. He found his own nomination and a photograph of himself taken a few months ago. How happy and innocent he looked then. He eyed the opposition in the programme and assessed his chances as being fair.

'Nervous, Yells? You look as sick as a dog,' Bill said.

'The BestMeat looks good,' Johnny replied.

'Nah! I've seen that line before. Don't worry: you'll get your plaque. Let me give you a tip: don't lift it with one hand, they're heavier than you'd think. It's the lead.'

Johnny turned to Penny who was looking around the room and enjoying the razzmatazz. He wondered if he loved her and for a brief moment he imagined that he did and he picked up her cool thin hand and kissed it. She looked proud of him.

'He's rather magnificent,' Penny said, indicating the tall, dark Wollard who always looked his best when it mattered.

Johnny shifted in his chair, irritated and intrigued at Penny's observation. The young woman accompanying Wollard looked at Johnny and he had the feeling that she knew about him and was now matching that reported description with the real him.

Bill suddenly cut across and asked Penny a question in attempt to charm. 'So is Johnny as nifty in bed as he is with a brief?'

Penny coolly considered this impertinence.

'He hasn't won any awards lately,' she said.

'Nice,' Bill Andrews said. 'Very nice.' He winked at Johnny. 'You'd better be careful. There are plenty of us award winners out here.'

Johnny suppressed a prudish desire to tell Bill Andrews to shut his mouth. He was surprised at Penny's response. Instead of telling Bill to mind his own business she had humoured the buffoon and insulted him to boot.

He felt an overwhelming disappointment towards all things: the false bonhomie, the self-congratulatory atmosphere, the innuendo. Bill's banter was tiresome, as was his knowing and predictable leering tone towards Penny. Johnny was relieved when the lights died down and Wollard made his way to the rostrum to get the proceedings under way.

At the platform Wollard seemed to grow, the applause

pumping him up larger than life. He did not lean upon the lectern but instead he stood beside it, lifting the microphone from its stand as though he had spoken to large numbers of people before. He was dressed in a dark, enviably tailored silk suit, a purple silk shirt done up at the top without a tie. His shoes were boots and black. He looked tall and still and nerveless, utterly confident of himself and of what he was going to say. He did not have to bang a gavel to bring on a quiet. Like certain creatures, Wollard instilled fear in people. His presence manufactured a silence; the silence you might find in an abattoir slaughtering lambs. His demeanour seemed to say: I know you will listen to me because what I have to say is important.

'We have in this building some of the most creative people in the land,' he began. 'People who can take a toilet roll, make it sing and have half the nation singing along with it. People who can make a nation believe there is a giant gulf between almost identical brands of cat food. People who can persuade a nation in the middle of a depression that their money is safe with one particular building society over another. People who can convince us that there is life after death.'

A knowing titter rippled across the room. Penny winked at Johnny.

'We are the people who dictate what the punter believes, what they buy, how they dress, where they go for their holidays and what they wipe their arses with. We tell them what baby food to eat when they're born and what policy to collect when they die. Some people take a dim view of this. We're a bad influence, they tell us. We have no morals, they say. Pah! What does morality have to do with it? There is only one kind of right and wrong that matters in this industry (and let's not forget that we are an industry): good work or bad work. A good idea or a bad idea. That is the only moral choice we need concern ourselves with.'

There was hearty applause for this.

'He's off,' Bill said.

'Persuading people to purchase products requires more than skill,' Wollard continued. 'It requires art. Give me a putrid soft drink with vile packaging to push on the public. That is a test. To stretch the boundaries of flattery; make a positive from a very real negative. If you can do it for the unlovely, the cheap, the lowly, the badly made, the tasteless, then you will succeed. We have to be as cunning, imitative and imaginative as artists. And, I believe that we are artists. Artists working in the most consistently creative medium that there is. In the next century our work will be exhibited in galleries and showcased at retrospective film festivals. We are the artists of the future.

'If you think I exaggerate then look around, talk to people. Ask them to think of the first image that comes to mind and it is very likely to be an image from a commercial or a poster. Ask a man in the street to whistle a tune and he'll sing you a jingle. You are responsible for creating these things. That, ladies and gentlemen, makes you artists.

'And like artists, we must live and breathe what we do. We must enjoy what we do. We must believe in what we do. We should certainly not be coy about it. Nor should we be ashamed. We must be proud of our efforts. We must reward our good work. If we are to foster creativity, if ideas are to ferment and bubble to the surface with any consistency, we must have a culture in which they can thrive. People must be made to feel that what they do is worthwhile, that it has value. That a poster for a jar of decaffeinated coffee is a thing of beauty as culturally relevant as a piece of sculpture, or that a commercial for a car is a work of art fit to rival the finest cinema has to offer.'

Wollard looked at the awards.

'That is why we have these. It shows that we care about what we do.'

Johnny's mouth was dry and he was aware of his breathing and a stiffness in his back and neck. He shifted his weight on the seat and found it hard to settle upon a happy position. Bill Andrews lit a cigarette. 'I could almost believe it. I almost feel like an artist,' he said. 'It's total bullshit, but it's necessary. It makes us all feel better.'

The applause rose and one or two people stood, then another and another until all around were standing. Johnny stood and clapped his clammy hands together. Wollard soaked up the applause like a dark sponge before handing over to the host.

The vast screen behind the stage came to life, the pointed heads of the Golden Plaques forming a silhouetted regiment in its bottom corner. The various categories were announced with each of the nominations being shown on the screen either in still or as film.

Johnny watched as the nominees were announced and he followed the winners as they walked to collect their Plaques wondering how he would walk should he win.

'You're going to win, I can feel it,' Penny said.

The early awards seemed to take an inordinate amount of time. There were more than fifty white envelopes on the table; one of which might have his name inside. The decision had already been made; there were people in this room who knew now who had won Best National Campaign; people who had played some part in defining his future, even his choice of home and car.

The compere tapped the microphone, 'And now to the National Poster Campaign category.'

Each of the nominees' posters was lit up on the screen. The BestMeat poster, which Bill Andrews had correctly observed as being derivative; a poster for the Stellen Fridge in an igloo; a poster for Shelldrake Chews in which famous buildings were constructed from the sweets; and in the bottom right of the screen, Smiling Jesus and his promise of life after death.

106

'And the winner is ... for ... LifeGen: copywriter: Johnny Ells, art direction: Bill Andrews.'

Johnny hardly noticed that the compere had misread his name, or that he was walking up to the stage, or that there were a thousand pairs of hands clapping his praises, or that the woman who presented him with the award was a well-known actress whose name he could not remember, or that Bill Andrews had come up with him when he had had nothing to do with the art direction. His eyes were fixed upon the screen that now showed his poster twenty times larger than actual size. As he received a kiss and a Plaque – which was heavier than it looked – he kept looking at the screen as though noticing some anomaly.

As he walked back he looked back. It wasn't the spelling: the words were the same. It wasn't the colours: they were true to the original; it was the face, still unsmiling, still definitely, absolutely, categorically not smiling.

By the time he was back at the table, the image had gone from the screen, replaced by the nominees in the next category. He put the Golden Plaque down and its dead weight made an unrefined clunk. Penny kissed him again and weighed the object in her hands before passing it around the table for each of them to hold, admire and remark upon.

Bill Andrews patted him on the back.

'You've arrived.'

'That wasn't the right image,' Johnny said.

'What?'

'That wasn't the LifeGen poster.'

'Looked like it to me,' Bill said.

'Ssshh. They're announcing the next award,' Penny said.

Johnny shook his head.

'They didn't show the original work,' he said, more to himself because none of the others were listening. He looked back at the screen even though he knew the image would not reappear.

Wollard joined them and congratulated Johnny. Johnny introduced Wollard to Penny and his boss bowed and kissed Penny's hand. Wollard then introduced the young woman as his sister and Johnny felt retrospectively different about the looks she had been giving him.

'You must be very proud,' she said to Penny.

Penny kissed Johnny to show that she was.

'I see that you aren't overjoyed at this little success,' Wollard said.

'He's trying to be cool,' Penny said, nudging Johnny's elbow.

'I think it shows that he has greater ambition,' Wollard observed.

Johnny let them reach their flattering conclusions.

The Golden Plaque had completed its circuit of the table and come back to him. He took it up and massaged its hard, cold edges, his fingers leaving little patches of sweat upon its surface. His hands were trembling and he put the award down.

Taylor's wife was watching him.

'Are you all right, Johnny? You look very pale.'

'I'm fine,' he said. 'It's the excitement of getting something you really want.'

SEVENTEEN

A vibrant Penny stood over him, tugging at the quilt. She was dressed smartly, as if ready for an important appointment. Johnny watched her bustle around the room, putting on her make-up. How ill he felt; how well she looked. Her skin was a honey colour and it glowed like the walls of a country village on a late summer's evening. She made an o with her lips and then pressed them together, sealing the lipstick.

'Come on!' she said. 'We have to be there at eleven.' Penny had no patience for malingering.

You are a malingerer. That is your problem.

'You're talking to yourself again,' Penny said.

'What?' Johnny said, surprised that she had noticed.

'You were mumbling, just now.' Penny passed him his shirt. 'You're not yourself are you?'

Damn right, Johnny thought. His self was back there somewhere, walking to work, not thinking, sidestepping oblivion with doing, not speculating beyond its means; his self was back there full of cheer and hope for the future.

He tried to picture himself as himself and he saw himself in his preteens, unaware of what his self was; then he saw himself being interviewed at WWW for the post of copywriter, green, keen and careless; then he was in the church of St Nicholas, looking at the icon of Smiling Jesus.

'Are you worried about the flat?' Penny asked.

'The flat?'

'Is it what you want?'

He had forgotten all about the flat. He was on the verge of making the most significant purchase of his life and he had forgotten all about it.

'I love the flat,' he said.

'Then what is it?'

He must say nothing. Particularly to rooted, earth-bound Penny. If she was worried about him talking to himself, she would think him insane for this symptom. But as he looked at the poster again, he could not deny that the smile was gone. He was sure of it now: in this poster here, the poster in the foyer, the cardboard cutout, the projected slide at the awards ceremony, he could no longer see the winning smile that he had encountered in the church of St Nicholas. But what does a successful young man do if he thinks an inanimate face printed on a poster is changing its expression without the aid of a lenticular device? Does he tell people about it and risk the consequence of being thought mad? Or, does he ignore it and tell himself that it isn't really changing, that it is just the result of a lively imagination and stress? If he's sensible, he'll ignore it. He'll put it out of his mind and maintain his own fixed grin for the world. He could not, would not, let such a curious phenomenon jeopardize things. Not now. Not now when he was about to write his first commercial; not now when he was about to buy a flat in Park West Gardens. Not now with a Golden Plaque glimmering upon his mantelpiece where there was room for several more.

It was a fault in the printing.

'Pen, would you say that he's smiling?' he asked, chattily, pulling on his trousers and selecting a tie to impress the building society with.

'We're late, Johnny, come on.'

'No really. It's important. The client isn't sure that he's smiling enough. We may have to change it.'

Penny looked at the poster.

'Of course he's smiling.'

Johnny went to the poster and traced a finger along the mouth of the Messiah. 'Is he smiling enough though?'

'Yes. Come on. Pull yourself together. We're going to be late.'

As they drove to the building society Johnny resolved to ignore it. He was not going to confront the issue any more because madness was surely a first cousin to such a contemplation. He felt the infectious exuberance of his girlfriend lift him. Penny was right: he should, in the very literal sense, pull himself together – knit back together the things that made him him. Like Penny, and like his old self, he should get excited about the prospect of a new home, of holidays, of going to the cinema, reading the latest novels: all the things that had once given him enjoyment.

Look at Penny, with her straightforward, getting-on-with-it face, her ability to enjoy the ephemera of life and take from it something meaningful, something that might make her happy and a better person. It's distasteful for you to begrudge her this, and arrogant. Enjoy life.

Penny talked about the property ladder and how glad she was to be stepping onto the first rung at last. But as Johnny pictured it he saw himself at the bottom looking up, unable to see what was at the top of the ladder and where it went to.

Where does it go?

'Sorry?' Penny asked him.

'What?'

'You just said something.'

Again Johnny was innocent of the fact that he had spoken his thoughts. He covered himself: 'I was just thinking.' But as he was saying it, he wondered why he was lying and not simply telling her that he was full of doubts.

'Why are you laughing?' he asked her.

111

'Because you look so earnest when you are talking to yourself.'

'I was just thinking out loud, that's all. I was thinking how much I'm looking forward to living in my own place – with you.'

The Spreading Oak Building Society seemed less like a place where large sums of money were borrowed and lent and more like a bright and colourful children's nursery. Perhaps the interior designers had been briefed to decorate the building in such a way that the customers were subconsciously reminded of their childhood and therefore forgot that they were making huge financial commitments that would last – in some cases – until they died. 'There is nothing to fear,' said the colour scheme, 'because the Spreading Oak Building Society has it all in hand, every eventuality covered and catered for: long-term savings, pension plans, projection charts. We have oracular powers of anticipation that will prepare you for every foreseeable event – even your own death.'

They were met by a Home Advisor called Miss M. Butler who led them to her office and closed the door. Behind her desk there was a wall chart which simply said 'Life' at the top of it. Below this there was a series of images which reminded Johnny of the evolution of man diagrams in his childhood encyclopaedias; instead of Cro-Magnon man moving to a more upright Homo sapiens, it showed a baby becoming a boy in school uniform, the boy becoming a fashion-conscious adolescent, the young man in a suit becoming a middle-aged man with a wife and children of his own, and finally an old man with his old wife, walking happily hand in hand to the next stage.

Beneath the figures there were appropriate captions: birth, school, job, family, house, business, retiring. 'We are with you at every stage of life,' said the Spreading Oak Building Society.

Johnny could see where he was now: somewhere

between the young man in the suit and the middle-aged man with the wife. And looking along the evolutionary path he imagined himself with Penny at the later stages. They could be that old couple stooping into their happy retirement, content with their lot, every question answered, every debt settled. And all because they had had the foresight to plan ahead and make provision.

Miss M. Butler congratulated them on their good sense in coming to the Spreading Oak Building Society and Johnny mentioned that he worked for the agency that did their advertising and that it would have been disloyal to have gone anywhere else. He knew, better than anyone, that he was in good hands here, he said, and Miss Butler smiled delightedly.

She then began to calculate the payments they would have to make every month, taking into account the life assurance policy, the endowment, the insurance against sickness and loss of earnings. She had their future at her fingertips, boxed off and protected.

Then Miss Butler told them about a particular mortgage protection policy, pointing to it on the form with her pencil held between thumb and forefinger.

'You can have a joint life-first death policy, which is a mutual benefit. So if one of you dies before the other the remaining partner is protected. It's just for extra peace of mind.'

'Who for?' Johnny asked.

Miss Butler repeated her patter.

'It gives peace of mind to know that should one of you die before the other . . .'

'But how does that give peace of mind? If I die first, I won't have peace of mind. I'll be dead.'

'I'm sorry, Miss Butler, he has a perverse sense of humour,' Penny said, keeping things running smoothly on the right tracks.

Miss Butler continued to explain the benefits and Johnny's gaze drifted back to the life chart. He followed the progress of the young baby from the beginning to the end of the chart, moving inexorably towards the end of the poster where the happy old couple walked to the stage that wasn't mentioned, the nothing for ever that Albert predicted. And yet the old couple were smiling without fear of its consequence, or of what it meant.

He felt his heart move unevenly in its cage. Nothing, not even Miss M. Butler and the elaborately constructed schemes of the building society, could stop him walking to the end of the abyss at the chart's edge.

'I don't feel sure about this,' he said.

The two women looked at him. Miss Butler with concern, Penny with disapproval.

'What is it you don't feel sure about?' Miss Butler asked.

'Everything,' Johnny said rubbing his temples in distress. I don't feel sure about anything.' The panic rose up in him, seeming to start at his middle and then spread to the tingling tips of his fingers; his breathing became lopsided.

'It's normal for people to feel apprehensive,' Miss Butler said, doing her job. 'That's why we're here: to reassure you and answer any questions you may have.'

'I'm not sure you can,' he said.

Johnny stood up to fight back the panic. He wanted to get out into the open air. He looked at the chart and into the helpful but clueless face of Miss Butler.

Penny stood bolt upright.

'It seems we need to work a few things out. Will you excuse us?' And she turned, not even looking at Johnny, and walked from the room, holding the door for him to follow. Johnny, unsure at first of what he had done to upset Penny, looked at Miss M. Butler as though she might explain; but Miss Butler said nothing and looked at Johnny as though he were a man who had lost the ability to discern the boundaries of normal, sane behaviour.

Outside Penny bore into him with a look powerful enough to wake a man from a coma.

'Snap out of it!' she said. 'Now stop it. If you don't want to sign it say so, but don't waste our time.'

People walked by and looked at them and looked away just as quickly. He wanted to address his concerns to the innocent pedestrians.

Damn you all. You're all very busy and in your bodies, getting on, doing. Don't you know that you are going to die some day, somehow, perhaps tomorrow? Maybe of a terrible terminal illness, perhaps in a sudden crush of metal and bone, or perhaps a slow, silent slipping away. Whatever, however. You're all going. Going, going, going, gone.

'I feel afraid, Pen,' he said. As he said it he was aware of saying it and that made him afraid too.

'You've got nothing to be afraid of,' she said.

For Penny, this breakdown was an unforeseen aberration but it was not going to spoil things. She was the rose-tinted girl and Johnny was not going to mess up her kaleidoscope by ruining the neat symmetrical patterns she had made for herself. She wanted a house full of windows and light and doors that opened and closed and that had hinges and she was going to get it.

'But I'm going to die,' he said.

'You are not going to die. Stop it, Johnny.'

'I am going to die. You are going to die.' How could she avoid the issue of her end? 'You must have thought about it, Pen.'

'I don't think about it. Why think about it?'

'Because it's definitely going to happen.'

'Look Johnny, you're not well. I don't know what it is. Ever since . . .' she checked herself.

'Ever since what?'

'You just . . . you just need a little help. Someone professional to talk to. But right now I want to sign this form. Take some deep breaths and calm down. That's it. Now, look at me. You're going to go back in and apologize to the lady. Then you're going to sign the form as though everything is all right.'

EIGHTEEN

Doctor Petterson's office was in his house which was located in a part of the city that Johnny and Penny could only aspire to live in. How Penny would have loved this house, Johnny thought to himself as he looked for the number of the door to see if it corresponded with the number on his scrap of paper that she had jotted down for him. It was quite definitely substantial, desirable and period. With its stucco decoration over the doorway, the light, high-ceilinged rooms and the clean brickwork, the doctor's house exuded a calm authority and Johnny was reassured by this. After all, it was paid for and constructed from the healing of sick people. How many restructured minds had contributed to its elevation and span, he wondered?

Doctor Petterson, a remarkably trim, well-dressed man, met Johnny and ushered him through to the capacious, light room that he had looked into and admired from the street. The doctor had an awkward manner and a reticence which Johnny thought appropriate for a man in his position. That reserve – which was, Johnny observed, a quality shared by Albert and all intelligent people – fostered an air of all-knowingness which was reassuring. Here was a man (judging from his house, his clothes, his book collection and his unfriendliness) who was clearly a very intelligent man indeed. Johnny was relieved to see that the doctor's face was not over-friendly and that his manner was free of false warmth. He didn't want someone to put their patronizing arm about him and hug him and say there, there. He wanted tough reasoning.

'You have a big garden,' Johnny said, his desire to sound normal, make small talk, getting the better of him.

The doctor said that he did and that Johnny was welcome to look at it if he wanted. Johnny went to the bay window and looked at the garden. It had one large tree which he couldn't identify and a carpet of early spring flowers. There was also an apple tree that looked fecund enough to produce an autumn crop good enough to fill Petterson's crystal fruit bowl there on the lacquered sideboard. Johnny walked back and took the chair that the doctor ushered him to. 'You have a beautiful place here.'

'Thank you. Why don't you tell me why you're here,' the doctor began.

Johnny started with the flu, his not feeling himself, the dreams, the fear of death and the arguments in his head. During this confession, which took some ten minutes, the doctor nodded encouragingly while keeping his hands clasped in front of his chin, as if he were praying to himself.

Johnny mentioned his father's death, then he told the doctor about Smiling Jesus, about the brief and the campaign. He was a little surprised that the doctor had not seen or even heard of the Smiling Jesus campaign, he must have been on the moon to have missed it; but then the doctor was clearly a busy man, too busy mending minds to notice something like that.

Then Johnny began to frame the words to describe the changing smile and he hesitated. It was plainly absurd; there was only one diagnosis for such a claim. He was afraid of the doctor's reaction. Once he had told him about the smile it was out; it was out and there were implications. There was a long silence and Johnny hoped the doctor would say something. After all, he'd given him enough to chew over. But Petterson could see that there was more to come and he said nothing.

The silence continued and Johnny waited for the doctor to say something, but Petterson was still looking at him, saying nothing. So he began to tell the doctor about the smile, how he had noticed it at home when looking at the poster on his bedroom wall, and then again at work and at the awards ceremony. All the time the doctor kept his quick-blinking eyes on Johnny and only his fingers began to move.

'Well. There it is,' Johnny said, making it all sound perfectly normal and feeling a great release at having told someone about it at last, particularly someone who might have a simple explanation.

For the first time in the session Petterson showed some expression in his face. He lit himself a cigarette, taking one rather clumsily from a packet of ten and lighting it unconvincingly, as though he had just learnt to smoke. He offered Johnny one and Johnny took it, thinking of a prisoner of war being offered a last smoke by his captor before being shot.

The doctor did not take his eyes from Johnny but he did not really look at him either. Johnny wanted to feel reassured by him and he looked into his wise and silent face and his eyes, quick-blinking like a tawny owl's, waiting for some sign, some encouragement that he had the answer, but still the doctor wasn't saying anything. Eventually he dropped his hands to his lap and spoke.

'How close were you and your father?'

'We weren't. I hardly saw him. I was sent away to school when I was seven.'

'Do you feel angry towards him?'

Johnny could feel himself being drawn a certain route by the doctor but he went with it.

'I think I do. Yes, I do. I hardly felt any emotion when he died. It was at his funeral that I got the idea for the campaign. The icon was there.'

Doctor Petterson scratched his chin. He looked to be piecing together some great puzzle.

'These voices. Are they recognizably your own, or do they seem like someone else's?'

'They're both me. I've always talked to myself, in my head. It's just that the voices have got stronger. I seem to be arguing with myself, constantly. It's wearing me down.'

'You say that you have had trouble sleeping. Have you been tired during the day?' This did not seem to have anything to do with it but maybe the doctor had a method.

'Yes. I've had trouble getting up. And at work my mind keeps drifting. I spend a lot of time thinking about death.'

There was a long silence again, the doctor putting together the different elements, with Johnny uncertain that the pieces he was feeding were the right ones.

'How is your mood? Are you able to enjoy yourself at all?'

The last rush of joy Johnny could recall having was in the church of St Nicholas, when he knew his idea was good.

'I feel afraid a lot of the time.'

'And when you see this . . . this changed smile . . . how have you felt?'

'Frightened as hell.'

Petterson was silent.

'What do you think it is, Doctor?'

Petterson then spoke more slowly but seemingly very sure of himself.

'Sometimes, under stress, it is possible for the subconscious to throw up an image that transcends reality. Stress can actually cause hallucinations. It may be that your unhappiness has caused a mind-projection: a psychotic experience so powerful that it has altered your sense of reality.'

Johnny looked at the doctor and his books around the walls and at the sheer opulence of the house, and thought who could argue with such a hypothesis? Wasn't every brick in the building cemented with right remedies? He had to be right. He was imagining these things and his fear was conspiring to bemuse his senses.

'This "changing smile" could well be a subconscious reaction to your father's death and the connection – in your mind – between the icon and that event. The loss of a loved one can trigger many things in our minds.'

'He wasn't a loved one.' There was a long silence again. Johnny felt that he had been steered into a box by the logic of the questions but that it was the wrong box. 'I'm not worried about him. I'm worried about me. I am afraid of death. I was never afraid of death before.'

'It's perfectly natural to fear death,' Petterson said, stubbing out his half-smoked cigarette. 'Circumstances – an illness or a depression – can easily exacerbate that fear.'

'But other people aren't afraid. Not the way I am. You're not afraid.'

The doctor fingered the stubbed cigarette in the white onyx dish, trying to stop it smoking. He gave the faintest of smiles, but there was nothing reassuring in that smile for Johnny, nothing that made him think that the doctor had the answer.

'Do you think there is a life after death?' Johnny asked.

Petterson coughed.

'No.'

'And doesn't that bother you?'

'Why should it?'

'But it must, a little.'

'I am resigned to it.'

'But you should be slightly afraid. You're going to die. You must think about it. You must . . . you must think about not being a doctor any more and not living in this beautiful house and not ever enjoying a cigarette ever, ever again or looking at those flowers and that tree or eating an apple from your garden?'

'Let's say, I have mastered my fear.'

'How?'

'By keeping busy.'

Discreetly, Petterson looked at the clock on the mantelpiece.

'Maybe that's my problem,' Johnny said. 'I haven't been busy. I've been thinking and not doing.'

'We are running out of time today; but why don't you come back next week, we can talk more about it then.'

Petterson pulled out a leather-bound appointment book and looked for a clear entry in the coming week. Johnny could see that Petterson had a full schedule. Clearly he was good at what he did.

'Shall we say next Thursday at three?'

'I'm busy then,' Johnny smiled.

Petterson looked again at the clutter of entries.

'I'm fully booked for the following week . . . unless you want to come Sunday. I sometimes do sessions on a Sunday morning. It's just an excuse to work harder.'

'To avoid the inevitable?' Johnny said.

'Can you come at eleven?'

'If I wake up, yes.'

'Here. This might help.' The doctor handed Johnny a leaflet entitled *Sleep Well* by Dr Petterson.

Johnny thanked Petterson and although he said he'd see him again he doubted he would. The doctor had failed to erase his deeper worry; he had, in fact, caused more obfuscation. And although he knew that these things were meant to take time, Johnny guessed that a thousand sessions with Petterson wouldn't yield the answer.

On the way to the station, he stopped to buy some flowers for Penny, keen to make up for the little incident at the building society. He selected a just-budding bunch of flowers, some twelve or thirteen of them. They would make a suitable gift, he thought. Perhaps they would be symbolic of a fresh start in him. He saw that one of the flowers was smaller than the others and that it lacked their colour. Perhaps it had failed to get enough light or nutrients and that had stunted its growth; maybe it was older than the rest of the bunch. Those other healthy flowers seemed to be willing him to pull out their feeble, withering friend.

He laughed at his propensity for seeing such things. It went with the job of course: dancing tomatoes, talking cats, conspiratorial flowers. Frowning Messiahs. As he pulled the failed flower from the bunch, the other flowers actually seemed to bow and thank him for removing the aberration. And there was no doubt about it: those flowers looked considerably better without their sick friend.

NINETEEN

Johnny was alone in the house, in bed, his eyes closed but his mind wide awake. He was trying to employ a method of sleep inducement recommended in Petterson's pamphlet, one based on the experience of a prisoner who overcame the frustration of captivity by imagining himself away from his cell, as a bird, making incredible journeys to places he was no longer able to see, recalling things in more detail than he ever could have remembered in his freedom.

Johnny tried to think of himself as a bird. He flew through the open window of his bedroom and out and up over the houses of Morton Road, towards the city. He flew up and up towards the thin layer of cloud, up and through to the dark blue and the stars, high enough to circle the entire city in a tight circle. Below him everyone was asleep. He was the only thing awake in the world. The wind changed and above him he could feel the shadow of thicker cloud blocking out the night sky, separating him from the stars. He began to descend, slowly at first and then faster as the weather changed. Soon his descent became a plummeting, the buildings below rising to meet him too quickly. He began to look for somewhere to land but everywhere he looked there seemed to be steeples stabbing the sky, waiting to impale him. He tried to hover but he had no ability to turn, his wings suddenly useless. He now fell at terminal velocity towards the sharpest spire of a church, his heart directly above its spike.

He sat up and put on the light.

He reached under his bed for a package: a brown bag with a book inside. He took the book from the bag and opened it. It was a little Bible he had found in a second hand bookshop. He had asked the shop assistant for the brown bag instead of the see-through carrier for fear of being seen with it. He had then smuggled the book into the bedroom as though it were contraband that might be used as evidence against him in a court of law. He was glad that he was alone in this house, glad that no-one was here to see him looking at this book. He could hardly bring himself to even imagine the reaction that an Albert, a Wollard or Doctor Petterson would have if they could see him with such a book. No doubt, they'd see it as an act of a desperate man, a weak man, unable to overcome something in his own strength.

Johnny? Are you getting religion?

He even read it a little desperately, like a gambler hoping to read straight away the jackpot answer to his question. As copy went it was turgid and he found it hard to follow the words, let alone believe them. The things he did read only served to make him more afraid. After only a short while he closed the book and put it in its bag and stuffed it under the bed.

He had not visited Doctor Petterson since the second session. The doctor had left a number of messages on the answer machine, each one growing more and more agitated than the last. Where was Johnny? Was he all right? Why hadn't he shown for his next appointment? It really was most disrupting for him to have patients fail to show up like this. Please would he call. He would now have to bill him for the cancelled session.

Petterson would have to wait. He didn't have the answers. Not really. He had some, it was true. He could explain most things coherently, deducing from Johnny's behaviour a diagnosis. But Johnny didn't want a diagnosis. He wanted to still the issue of his absolutely definite demise within the next hundred years and the total uncertainty of his whereabouts thereafter, for one. The doctor had little to say on this subject.

Last night, he had called Edson. He now wished he could have erased that moment. Thankfully, he had not said too much. He had garbled about the campaign and its effect on his mind and stopped short of uttering the words that would have had Edson round here in minutes to join him in prayer. He had lost heart or rather he had, perhaps, found his senses, managing to invent a convincing line about being a little drunk and over-worked and needing to let off steam. He had then backed out before giving Edson the opportunity to say anything.

Johnny got up, feeling that he was being watched. Maybe there were cameras in the room, relaying all this – even his thoughts – to Penny, to Albert, to Petterson, to Wollard. He looked for devices of subterfuge, around the walls and under the bed, and in the heels of his shoes. He walked around. He went out onto the landing, to Albert's room and switched on the light.

A dry-cleaned suit hung behind the door, still in its polythene wrapping. At the window there was a desk and a computer and above that a shelf with several thick volumes on various branches of law. On the desk there was a notepad with a list of names on it. He looked behind him even though he knew full well that Albert was two hundred miles away in a hotel, sleeping soundly.

The names on the pad were spaced evenly around an oblong that presumably represented a table. Johnny recognized all the names except for one female. They were friends of Albert's and the list looked to be a guest list for a dinner party. Penny was there, represented by a P; Albert by a Me and, at one end of the oblong, there was a J? A J with a question mark.

Johnny stared at that question mark and little pins and needles prickled in his spine. It was only a single piece of punctuation but it contained a whole case against him, a spectrum of accusation.

J?

Was it a question as to whether to invite him to the party?

Perhaps there were others he might want to invite. After all, Albert did live with Johnny.

This was possible but why then did Penny not have a question mark after her name? He wouldn't have invited Penny without him.

Was it a more specific query as to whether to seat him at the end of the table?

But why just him?

Or was it, as he suspected, a more serious question as to whether Albert thought Johnny was fit to invite? That question mark might well have contained all Albert's worst fears and prejudices. It was a 'what is wrong with Johnny?' question; an 'I'm not sure about Johnny' question. An 'is Johnny getting religion?' question.

Albert was worried that Johnny might embarrass his friends; that he might introduce unsuitable and embarrassing subject matter at the dinner table. He had, after all, expressed concern at the way Johnny was looking these days.

You can't blame him for that.

In Albert's mirror Johnny could see the features of the ranter: his hair was thinning and unbrushed, he was pale with inactivity and thinking. He hadn't shaved for weeks and a wispy malingerer's beard had sprouted. No. He couldn't blame Albert for his little question mark. His behaviour had put an electric fence of danger about him, created the wide berth that people gave to madmen. If Johnny was Albert he would have written that question mark. In fact, he might not have trusted himself enough to put his name on the list at all.

TWENTY

It was raining hard and a number of sensibly clad people raised their eyebrows at the sight of a shambling, pre-occupied young man without a raincoat wandering the city streets. The rain was falling upon his unkempt hair and he was muttering to himself as though engaged in some intense polemic.

Like anyone having an argument, he was unaware of what was going on around him: of the people and what they were thinking; of the rain which was cold and spite-ful; and the billboards displaying new advertisements which he might once have appreciated for their in-references and clever puns. His mind was in dispute: there was an unruly parliament in there and he could no longer call it to order.

This is pitiful. What do think you are going to achieve by this?

Peace of mind.

Piece of crap. You should be writing that commercial. Do you expect it just to write itself?

I want confirmation. Certainty. I want certainty.

Oh, you're confirmed all right. Certified. Out of what mind you think you have.

Shut up. I know what I need.

Do you honestly think that the curve of paint on a canvas is going to set everything right? What you need is a damn slap in the face. This is an embarrassment.

Johnny quickened his step in order not to think, but at every other stride he trod on his undone lace. He stopped to tie it and leant over his boot.

Look at your boots. Those pitiful excuses for footwear at the end of your legs; look at the split developing there. The stitching is coming away just like you: I can see your sock. Look there. It's your sock sticking out like a tongue: nerny nerny ner ner.

I can get them fixed.

Not at this rate. One minute you can afford a hundred square feet of slate over your head, the next you won't be able to afford an umbrella.

In the window of a shop he caught sight of someone he vaguely recognized. He was repelled by the figure, looking like that, standing like that, dressed like that in the middle of a downpour. But looking closer at the face reflecting back he saw that it was his own.

Look at you. Yes, you!

Johnny noticed the rain for the first time because it had got into his collar and down his neck, the way it had done when he was a boy and wore shirts that were always too big for him. He shivered at the thought of himself as a boy in some warmer world and the innocent 'then' contrasted with the nasty 'now'. He pressed on, fixing a determined expression and shaking his head to get the rain from his face.

St Nicholas was still there. Still tall and grey but more reasonable now. The scaffolding had been taken down and the spire pointed purposefully to the sky. The appeal fund notice board showed that the target of £100,000 had been achieved.

He went to his father's shiny, granite headstone and stood looking at it. It showed the name Edward Yells, and the dates. There was no other information. Would his own life come to this, his achievements abbreviated to a few words on a stone slab?

> *Here within lies Johnny Yells.*
> *Oh really – what did he do?*
> *He wrote some lines for companies,*
> *You might have heard of one or two.*

Inexplicably Johnny started to cry, a sudden but profound weeping that hurt him in the middle of his chest. He wasn't sure if it was for his father, or if it was for himself; but he saw his father as he had been that day at the airport, the last time he had seen him breathing, and he wanted to remember what warmth, if any, he had felt for him in that snatched meeting. He looked at the headstone and wondered if his father could hear him. Where was he?

Maybe, maybe if there was truly something beyond this, something lasting and eternal, then he might be free from this earthbound worry. If he could, just for a moment, imagine the truth, feel the truth, know the truth of an eternal existence (he tried now) then he might find the peace of mind that eluded him. Kneeling there in the rain he tried, without having the means to believe it, to picture it, but there was no picture, only nothing.

He went to the door of the church and as he walked under the porch the rain stopped falling on his head. He felt the water sponging into his exposed sock and he bent down and poked a finger in there. Then he stood up and twisted the cold iron ring of the door and felt the latch lift but when he pushed against the door he banged his head.

Closed for business. What are you going to do now? Break in?

Johnny tried the door again twice and then went to the other side of the church where he found another locked door. At the back of the church there was a modern extension to the vestry and a window that looked as though it might be open. Ignoring the driving rain he climbed on to the ledge and pushed at the window. It was locked.

For a while he stayed there, balancing against the window, his mind empty of thought and no signal of will telling him what to do next. He saw that if he broke the small top window he might reach around and open the big window and let himself in. Without telling himself to, he broke the small window and reached around and lifted the holed catch and let himself into church the hard way.

The violence of breaking in and the silence after the noise of the glass shattering made him suddenly more alert to the world outside himself and he crouched down in the vestry amongst the cassocks and robes waiting to see if he had been heard. But it was quiet and the quiet encouraged him and he moved through to the main building, emerging into a church which was filled with flowers in vases and cruses, hanging urns and tied in wreaths and smaller bouquets. Johnny was excited and glad that he had broken in even though he knew it to be wrong in some way.

He passed the portraits of Pale and Chubby Jesus, their expressions unchanged, the same as they were the day he last saw them. He could hardly wait now to look at the smiling face of the icon. He looked ahead at the space on the wall where there was an oblong stain of paint, the print of where the painting had formerly hung.

There was no doubt that it wasn't there, his eyes were not deceiving him. It must have been moved to another part of the church, to a more prominent place perhaps; and he walked back along the nave where he thought there was paint on the slate floor. He hopscotched to avoid it; and then he stopped when he saw that the paint was also on his clothes and that it wasn't paint but that it was blood.

He ignored the blood for the time being; there would be time to sort that out once he had found what he was looking for; but what he was looking for was not here and he let out a small cry of despair. He felt suddenly faint and he sat down upon a carved, backless seat just behind a blue rope barrier. He wanted to get away from himself but he couldn't because he was housed inside himself for good and any improvements and extensions to himself had to made on what shaky foundations and material he had.

Help me, please.

'I'm afraid the church is closed,' a low, firm voice said. 'And you're sitting on a valuable artefact. The rope is there to protect it.'

A man in a black cape, with a white dog collar, looked at him from the correct side of the blue rope. His voice was soft and firm like a competent teacher's and he was small and neat and clipped rather like a toy breed of dog.

And this year's winner: Vicar. Beautifully groomed, excellent pedigree, sired out of Bishop.

Johnny laughed at his private and tangential joke.

The man looked afraid of something and the blood leaving his face made his skin blotchy. Johnny recognized him from the funeral but the vicar looked at Johnny as though he had never seen him before in his life.

Johnny looked at his still bleeding hand and the blood was thick and brown and already coagulating on the floor around his feet.

'Perhaps I can get you a bandage for that,' the vicar said, speaking calmly, the way people did to unpredictable persons. 'Why don't you sit there and I will get you a bandage and perhaps a towel for your hair. You look wet through.'

'Like a dog,' Johnny said.

'Maybe you would like a cup of tea?'

'Spare me the price of a cup of tea,' Johnny repeated, finding this word association a simple and satisfying way to converse.

'I'll just go to the vestry, you stay there on the bench,' the vicar said, backing away nervously and not taking his wide, frightened eyes from Johnny.

Valuable bench. Protected species. Rare breed. Artefact. Arts a fact.

Johnny's mind reeled on like a drunk thesaurus.

The vicar returned with two dish cloths and a towel. Johnny hung the towel over his head and breathed in the smell of wet dog.

'We had a dog once,' Johnny said, thinking he'd made a valid connection.

The vicar tied one of the cloths around Johnny's hand and then mopped the blood from the floor with another.

'You're a man of the cloths,' Johnny said and he shivered and felt sad as the vicar cleaned up the blood and tourniqueted his hand.

'You are wet through. Put this over your head.'

'Where have you put him?'

'Put who?'

'You've put him somewhere. Is he behind that curtain?'

'Who do you mean?' the vicar asked; he was sweating now.

'You know who I mean. Smiling Jesus.'

'It was sold to raise money for the steeple.'

Do you trust this peddler of obscure myths and half mysteries? He's lying. He's got him somewhere up his cassock, he's put him somewhere just to stop you seeing him because he is smiling. He wants you to think you're mad.

'You're not hiding him from me are you?'

'I think you should sit there while I get a doctor. That cut will need to be looked at. Just wait here and I'll go and call one.'

'No! Don't go. Don't go. You must help me. I need to know something. I need to know what happens when we die. Where do we go? You must know. You bury people, you help them on their way. Where do we go?'

The vicar seemed unable to remember, like a travel agent who's never been to the country he sells holidays to.

'You want me to write an advertisement. Let me think. No. Wait. Yes. Vicar, I've got it. Get an afterlife. For

133

Eternal Life Assurance talk to Vicar. Because. Because
. . . tomorrow you could be dead. I don't want to die,'
Johnny said.

'You're not going to die. Just let me get a doctor.'

'No! Wait. Just tell me one thing,' Johnny said, feeling
weak now and wanting sleep. 'Was he smiling when
they took him away? Jesus?'

'I am sure he was,' the vicar said.

'That's all I wanted to know, Your Priestliness. That's
all I wanted to know. Thank you for your kindness.
You've saved me a lot of sleepless nights. Are you sure
now? Sure he wasn't sneaking a little frown when they
took him away? Sure you were looking hard enough?
He's a sneaky one that Smiling Jesus.'

The vicar did not reply, he went to make the phone
call. Johnny drifted and woke up hardly aware that he
had been awake before that little rest. He had fallen
asleep right there on the bench. The bloodstain had
formed a tidemark at the edge of the bandage, blotting
it from white to red.

The vicar was still the other side of the blue rope and
Johnny looked at his face, maybe hoping to see something of the face he was looking for in it, just a sign of
reassurance.

'If I die what will happen?' Johnny asked.

'You won't die,' the vicar said. 'But you have cut yourself quite badly.'

'I don't want to die,' Johnny said.

The vicar looked around, listening out for something.
'They'll be here soon,' he said.

'He's not happy with me, that Jesus,' Johnny said,
slurring now. 'You think he'll have a mansion for me?'

The vicar had half an ear elsewhere.

'What?'

'He's got mansions, hasn't he?'

There was the sound of a siren and the vicar said that
he would let the doctor in. The footsteps of all the doctors

134

were loud, the clicks of their steel heels echoing on the slate floor. Johnny saw that the vicar's expression had changed from quite friendly to a sterner look. Johnny tried to cheer him and remind him. 'When there are smiles there are miles and miles of smiles. But when you frown there will be frowns all around the town,' he said. But the vicar didn't seem to agree with this proverb at all and he stood back and let the doctors through and Johnny saw that they were not all dressed as doctors usually were and that they were handling him with a roughness that seemed out of place in a church and inappropriate towards someone in need of urgent medical attention.

TWENTY-ONE

They've taken him away. They're taking me away. Where are we going? Where is he? Have you got him, gentlemen? Unhappy isn't he? Smiling for years until he saw me. Don't look so concerned there. When you die there will at worst be nothing for ever and that has to be something to not worry about because you can't worry about nothing. Believe me; you will never die. There's Life after Death. Talk to LifeGen. Everything all right at home is it? Got your life assurance? Good. I expect you get a good one from the ambulance service. What about your health? Got that covered? In the event of illness break glass. Just break the glass. Mind you don't cut yourself now. Look at me: twenty-nine stitches: one for every year of my life, one for every year of my wife. A stitch in time saves . . . oh, I don't know what it saves. Save our souls. Save my sole, save my boots, mend my boots, bend my boots, bend my mind, mend my mind. It is cold and I am cold but I am also hot. I'm an artist, gentlemen, and that, as you well know, explains why I blow hot and cold. Did you know I was a world-famous artist? You have probably seen my work without realizing it because it's 'part of the very fabric of society'. I am an artist of the Twenty-first Century. This is a brainstorm – anything goes. Write it all down. Are you writing all of this down? Could be an award-winning campaign in it. Have you seen Him anywhere? Have you? I was just talking with vicar back there and he says He's gone to auction. Made me cry. He actually made me cry. Only the finest art moves people that way. He's crying, too – wherever He is. I know it. Oh please stop crying, Messy. Stop it now, please. Can I trouble you for a handkerchief, chief? Let me have that hanky panky. Where's Penny? In for a penny out for ten thousand pounds. What's that? Don't think I can't hear every damn thing you're saying. Who are you calling there? Are you calling Him, Him on the other side, making sure everything's ready, that I've got my room booked in the eternal rest home? I want a nice view. I want a bloody marvellous view – one I can stare at for ever and ever and not get bored. What's that? Section? There's a section there? One Three Six. Is that my room number? Book me in. I want my mansion. Better have a good view. All this blood: I must surely die soon. Convey. Conveyance? Place of safety. Safety pins. Pin me down. But don't hurt me, you brutes. God I am cold. God I am. God I. I. I am. I am God. I am God cold. What's that you're saying? Stop whispering. Clang Association. Is that the bell-ringers? Are you a doctor? Is that my end you're tolling? Had to come soon. Can you give me a jumper to wear there? I don't want to be cold for ever. Unless it's hell where it'll be hot according to the brochure. What? Next of kin? Are you telephoning my family? I'd better have a word now that I am off to the other place for ever. Let me speak to my father. See what it's like over there. Won't you pass the phone? I'd like to see, to speak to him before I get there. Father? Is that you? Hello? Hello? Is that you? Why don't you speak to me? Is this line engaged? It must all be jammed up with all those people trying to get through. My clothes aren't that colour. Is blood brown? Don't be a fool, man. It's the running dye from my wet boots. My arm. My arm. What's that you're giving me? Something to calm me down? You want me to take that do you? In my mouth. Like this. Mmmm. Is that it? Am I dying now? Is that my life flashing before me? Roll up, coming soon, showing now: your life in less than a second. I'm going to heaven, gentlemen. This is it, I believe. Believe and it will never be it. Believe in him and you'll never die. I am cold. I am very cold.

Johnny was in darkness; and then, although he could not see, he felt the darkness close in around him and he was afraid and the darkness seemed to swallow him with its black mouth and chew him up in its black stomach but it couldn't quite digest him because he was aware of himself, holding on to the thing that was him – his sense of self; and he thought that he must hold on to the self because that's where his life was. And he remembered that he'd thought that before. He thought of what he was but it seemed he was only made up of a medley of memories each projecting an image of mixed clarity into what was still his mind and he knew that he was not dead yet because in death he would surely know for sure either way: either not know anything because he was nothing, or know for sure because he was something; but he was in the nether regions, a twilight of flickering thoughts, and he listened out for himself and he could hear, like a drum that reverberates in a room with low ceilings, the beat of his life; he listened to it intently and ever so slightly its throb diminished and slackened off and he thought that if he remembered himself again the boom might increase so he thought of himself again and he was walking to catch his train and everyone travelling with him was someone he knew and, according to how well he knew them, they took up positions on the train. And he was saying to all of them how cold and tired he was and that letting him sleep would have the most wonderful effect on him if only they'd stop talking to him. Albert was there looking dark and distinguished and he was remonstrating with a policeman, explaining to that man – in enunciation so clear that the policeman's jaw dropped – that there had been a terrible mistake and that his friend needed help, that he must be taken to a place of greater safety. Albert wore a suit that might double up for the funeral should it come to that; so clever, so erudite, so calm, his reason rolling on fast-moving well oiled frictionless tracks racing him to utter certainties. And there's Penny and she too was persuading him to stay awake and do his very best; he couldn't throw it all away now. Not now, Johnny! Come on!

Johnny kept moving through the carriage away from the people he knew best until he could hardly hear their shouts and demands and cries; he went on and into the next carriage which was moving and shaking a little from side to side and the view ahead was a staggered one through the connecting ends of the carriages and the windows ahead were getting smaller and smaller and darker and darker and Johnny thought that the light down there must be the tunnel they talk about: the one that those near-death travellers experience and he thought it a crass way to enter another life but none the less he kept a sharp eye out and he pressed on through the train past everyone he'd ever met, all seated in a perfectly ordered chronology of affection. They all said something to him as he walked past them but he didn't 'hang on in there', as one of them suggested, he pressed on to the end of the carriage which was itself moving at some speed through the tunnel. There were advertisements in strips either side and people were looking at them and he looked at the products that were being advertised and damn they were attractive and worth spending at least a part of a lifetime chasing, but he pressed on aware that there was someone behind him trying to haul him back, pulling at his shirt-tail. 'Hold on to yourself,' they called. But as he tried to think again this idea of himself seemed to slip from him until he couldn't remember himself; and he cried out because he knew now that he was close to death.

Pretty soon he knew he would be at the end and he started to look for his father – he must be there somewhere. He walked into the final carriage which was quite the darkest in the line and he nodded to the people there, some of whom he had been at school with. Johnny wondered how he could be this close to death and remember people he cared little for with such clarity. He could see the back of the carriage with the window looking out the back on to a track which could not be seen and he looked out of the window into the black, expecting there to be a gradation, a hierarchy of blackness, but the blackness was all-pervading now and he thought 'there is nothing'. And he took a privileged glimpse of that blackness and thought he might step into it without fear. There was no Smiling Jesus; there was no gateway; no tunnel; darkness reigned and there was no doorway and no-one greeting him, no life after death, even though he had been told by someone to expect this: hadn't it been advertised once? (I'd better get my refund.) And then he knew that all the hopeful reports of a tunnel leading to light were bogus, they were just the confused flickers of the brain. Just think of the thousands, perhaps millions, of people that will die with expectation drawing out their last breath, he thought. There they will be believing there's something more (because who wouldn't want to believe it?) and then, as their last breath became part of the atmosphere, and their synapses began to short and fuse, they would see little lights flickering which they'd mistake for the pathway to the next life but which were, in fact, the last requests of the brain. For a fraction of time they might see Smiling Jesus greeting them with that smile and the light would go out before they knew that that image was simply their memory's last projection.

Looking at that dark he thought he'd best get back to the front and let all those people know what he'd seen; they ought to know that there was nothing. Spurred by this reason not to slip away into the tranquil and suddenly friendly nothing he generated the light needed to see his memories. He saw himself getting dressed and then he was crying and then he was kissing someone. Then those thoughts of that person blurred and blacked out and he half hoped again for that opening to some other place to appear and lead away from this enfolding darkness. He walked back through the carriage and all the same people were looking at him, as though wanting to know just what it was he had seen back there at the end of the carriage, and they patted his back and clamoured to ask him and for a time this slowed him up and he couldn't move. He wanted to tell them but he had to get to the front, to the driver, and tell him first, so he fought them off, telling them they'd all know soon enough and he pressed on back to the front of the carriage. And then, in the next carriage, he looked at the advertisements above the people in the strip lighting, adverts for cars, for toothpaste, for meals in packets and for mobile telephones – real certainties, tangible, solid goods that you worked for and dreamed of and looked at and then bought, and Johnny heard himself say how honest and true a striving it was to look at these adverts and want what was in them. These people should look to the advertisements instead of worrying what was at the back of the train. He could see now that these advertisements were here to stop people from going to the back of the train to look. And the ones who read the advertisements were the happy ones. And they were right to do this because there really was nothing there at the back of the train: no heaven, no hell, no Jesus, nothing.

And a man in black ticket inspector's uniform was dispensing the tickets and Johnny thought he should get his ticket quickly so he got off after him but the man remained just ahead of him. He followed him back to the front of the train, pushing through and calling out 'Ticket! I want my ticket,' but no-one seemed to hear him, let alone the ticket man. He thought: I must get to the front of the train and tell the people there and the driver to keep going and he kept going back to the front. He pushed into the last carriage – the one attached to the engine – and he could hear the beat of himself and he looked at the people he knew in this carriage who were waiting on his every breath and he smiled at them

141

as if he had not seen them in years and he saw that he had to get his ticket first and so he carried on still to the very front of the train where he could see the back of the inspector's head, and he pulled his shoulder and he turned and it was Wollard.

Up ahead the station was coming into view and Johnny had to get that ticket. Wollard pressed the buttons on his dispenser and a great golden ticket stuttered out of it and Johnny pulled it and ran on to the engine where the driver looked out and he touched the driver's head telling him to stop and as he reached to touch the head he actually felt it and, because he knew it was real, he pulled his hand back at once. He looked ahead of the driver through the window and he saw more darkness and the darkness was becoming grey and there were shapes and he became conscious of things: material objects, and they were reassuring objects and then, as if emerging from the tunnel, his ears popped and he saw in the clear of day that these objects were a bed, a glass of water, hard cotton sheets up over him and a woman in white and he felt glad that he was here and not back there at the cold end of the train looking back at the hurtling black nothing which lay beyond his life.

PART THREE

'New, Improved Johnny Yells'

TWENTY-TWO

A smell of disinfectant and floor polish mingled with the starchy hit of overlaundered sheets. There was the tiss of muffled music, the tinkle of metal on metal and a crinkling of busy, bustling clothes. Sheets itched against his skin and there was something wrapped around his wrist and arm. He opened his eyes and saw a woman leaning over and tucking in a sheet and blanket which were covering his legs. The woman was wearing a white tunic, her hair was tied up severely and a silver cross dangled from her neck flashing in the sun filtering through a skylight above him. The woman – whose badge said Nurse Martin – turned and took a pillow from a metal trolley, puffed the pillow and placed it behind his head.

So, here it is. The promised and predicted heavenly mansion: a little darker than I imagined although it has generous proportions, which, of course, I shall need if I am going to live here for ever. These white-coated men and women might be angels, but there are blue ones, too. What? Am I to share my mansion with other people? What if we don't get on? What's that smell? Like a cross between a prison and a cheap hotel.

'There you are,' the nurse said.

A little while ago (he could not say when exactly) he had wondered if he was journeying to the next life. He looked up now and thought that perhaps his bumpy passage had necessitated some repairs. Perhaps he had made it, but only by the hairs on his chinny, chin, chin, singed at the edges, his fingernails bleeding (there still seemed to be blood there).

The ward was filled with the light of morning, a light so warm and clear that it seemed it might improve the condition of the broken and bruised in their beds. Beside his bed there were flowers and cards that he could not recall being put there. He felt the appreciation for all things that comes with near escapes: the ephemera of a breath, the rising of his stomach, the whistle of air in his nostrils.

As the nurse fussed about him he took delight in her little eccentric movements and the sound the sheets made as they were flipped beneath the bed and given the symmetry of a perfect corner.

'That's beautiful,' he said.

'Thank you,' she said. 'We want you looking good for the doctor, don't we?'

The nurse pulled the curtain around the bed for privacy and to protect the other patients from noise. She wore a perfume he recognized – one that was unlikely to be retailing beyond the natural world.

'N'Oubliez,' he said, his voice cracked and dry.

Nurse Martin stopped her primping and tucking.

'You haven't lost your sense of smell then,' she said.

'That's the ad where the blinded prince returns to his castle to find several ladies claiming to be his princess,' he said, reminding himself.

'I haven't seen that one,' she said.

'He recognizes his princess from the perfume.'

From the composite of familiar, earthy smells and sounds, and the dull dawning ache in his arm, it was becoming clearer to him that he was still him, still living.

'How is your arm?'

He lifted it to see a perfectly applied lint dressing covering a width of his limb from the wrist to the elbow. The ache became a hot soreness.

'It itches.'

'It was a deep cut. Don't rub it. There are twenty-nine stitches there.'

He couldn't remember how this had come about just yet; he decided to let the nurse piece his story back together. 'Did you put this bandage on?'

She nodded. 'Whoever put that other bandage on you forgot to tie it.' Dimly, he remembered a man tying his arm while he lay back, his feet raised above his head which rested on a stone cold floor.

'Your clothes have been washed.'

A soft tower of freshly laundered clothes lay atop his bedside cabinet. He poked the pile to test the softness, the whiteness.

Only Turbo Blue will do, make you feel like new, like new.

A man with a nameplate that said Doctor Evington poked his head round the curtain. He looked tired but cheerful and he seemed pleased by what he saw.

'You look better. Colour in your cheeks.'

Johnny was still but he knew that it would be an effort to move.

'I am tired.'

'That's to be expected. You lost a great deal of blood.'

Johnny was hoping for more information. 'How much?'

'Enough to put you in danger. It was close,' he said. He seemed unworried by Johnny's condition and talked to him as though he were a man in the best of health.

'Close?' Johnny said.

'Let's just say that it was a good job they got you here when they did. You were at death's door.'

Now there's an interesting door to open.

'How "close" was I?'

'You were unconscious.'

'Did I die? I mean technically, for a minute.'

That would have been long enough to get a good glimpse at eternity; long enough for someone on the other side to welcome you to the next world – if there was someone there.

147

The doctor didn't answer him. He looked at his clip-board and examined the data.

'Let's have a look at the arm.'

He untied the dressing and peered at the long, jagged scar, red but clean. He pointed to a vein running up the arm from the wrist where the cut was particularly jagged. 'That's the part that did the damage. It looks good. The stitching will have to stay in for another week, but the bandaging can come off tomorrow . . . Let's have a listen to that heart.'

The cold disc tickled. The doctor listened and nodded as though hearing a bright symphony.

'So, did I die, Doctor?'

The doctor thought about what he was going to say, caught perhaps between his desire to tell the truth and need to protect the patient. 'It's all right,' Johnny said. 'I'd like to know.'

'Your heart rate dropped very low; it was barely discernible when you were brought in. The ambulance crew said they had to resuscitate you. The notes don't tell me whether your heart actually stopped.'

'Is a resuscitation the same as a resurrection?'

'People can be "brought back to life".'

Johnny looked carefully at the doctor, wondering if he might venture a metaphysical question. Doctors deal in life and death. Why not?

'Have you ever had any patients who "came back" from the dead and talked about what was on the other side?'

Doctor Evington smiled and tutted. 'There are cases but none of them has ever been on my shift.'

'Do you think there's life after death?'

'There may be. But there's no proof. People do see these "near deaths" as genuine conscious experiences but the likelihood is that the sensations are organic responses of the brain.'

'When do you think I can leave the hospital, Doctor? I have a job to get back to.'

'I'd like to keep you in until Sunday. We can look at those stitches then.' The doctor wrote something on the board.

'What are you writing?' Johnny asked.

Doctor Evington showed Johnny the words he had just written: 'Patient improved'.

TWENTY-THREE

Penny appeared bearing gifts. She had brought fruit and books and some post. She kissed him and hugged him and he breathed in her musky scent. She then held his good hand.

'You look a lot better,' she said.

'I feel better.'

'I brought some books. And lots of people have been asking after you.'

'Work?'

'I spoke to that Judy. She was very sweet; wanted to know where to send flowers. Said to send her love.'

'What did you tell them had happened?'

'I said that you had had an accident.'

And it was true. He had. An accident of thinking as potentially damaging as any car crash. Penny caressed the skin around the scar on his arm and then she looked at him intensely as if he had been away for a long time and got lost in a country of murky mists and myths.

'Johnny. What did happen? What were you doing at that church? Albert said they thought you had broken in or something. Is that true?'

It was clear that she didn't know and this was fine news. As the dark glass lifted from his own memory he began to recall his actions with a vague feeling of shame.

'I spoke to Doctor Petterson,' Penny went on, gently, as though he were a delicate flower. 'I never realized how upset you were about your father. I didn't realize.'

This was fine news, too. He was grateful for the plausible psychological alibi of his father's death. It comfortably explained his actions and, to some degree, it excused them. He did not need to dispute this version of events. He would keep the embarrassment of his 'seeking', his brush and flirt with religion's lure, to himself. Perhaps that was it after all: his repressed grief surfacing. Better to let Penny and the others think this. He squeezed her hand.

'I think I buried my feelings for too long about Father. I really didn't allow myself a period of time in which to grieve properly. When I went to the church I thought in some crazed way that I might find him there. That I might find some answer. I was angry. And crazy. I'm sorry, Pen. I can hardly believe that was me behaving that way. It seems like a different person back there.'

'It's not your fault,' she said. 'I should have been more sensitive. When you were talking about death and worrying about it I should have made that connection earlier.'

Johnny had the feeling that he had got away with something. He had, through his strange actions, come close to losing his job, his friends, his girlfriend, his home and his life. He had contracted the near-fatal virus of superstition and had got over it. He should thank whoever it was he should thank for the narrow escape and get back to being normal again. Normal. That was the elusive condition he needed to catch.

'Tell me about the house,' he said.

Penny seemed to relax and brighten at the mention of her happiest theme.

'We can move in in two weeks. The papers have all gone through. This is what we need.' Her faith in the medicine of real estate was undiminished. She continued to talk about her plans for the flat and he listened to her and felt glad for the material comfort that awaited him. He almost wanted to get out of his bed now and walk out into life again. Life. He could feel it now, out there,

151

waiting for him, buzzing, busying, reproducing, produc-
ing, waxing, waning, ebbing; open-armed life with its
equal potential for loss and gain, smack and caress, resuscitation and deathblow. Lovely full-bodied, living life.

He stroked her arm and listened to her without paying
attention to the words, but simply to the fact that she
was there and that he was alive to know it. How lovely
it all sounded to him. This was happiness he could trust.
To think that he had had the arrogance to think himself
superior to her for wanting the security of a home. While
she had kept her feet on the ground, he had flown in
ever ascending circles above and out of his mind, looking
for something that did not exist, wearing himself out
until he had crashed back down to earth. He squeezed
her hand tightly for several seconds and thought of being
with her for the rest of that life he was going to live
when he left this place.

'Wollard telephoned. He was very anxious to hear how
you were. I laid it on a bit without going into great detail.
I said that you nearly died – which isn't exactly a lie. He
was very kind. He insists that you take a holiday before
you come back. He said that Taylor would look at the
commercial, or something.'

The mention of Wollard and work galvanized Johnny's
competitive instinct.

'Can you do me a favour?' he asked her.

'Anything.'

'Get me some paper.'

Penny looked at him in a mock cross way. 'You know
you should be resting.'

'Just this one favour.'

She went to find some, whilst Johnny looked for the
Biro in the bedside drawer. He sat up, closed his eyes,
seeing the whole thing, the whole commercial, in exact
detail. Penny fetched a hardback book to rest the paper
on and sat next to him.

'I'm going to dictate something to you.'

'You're mad, Johnny. What is this for?'

'It's a commercial. It's important that you get this to Wollard, Pen. Can you get it typed up and faxed to him by tomorrow?'

'I'll try.'

'No. Promise me you'll fax it tomorrow.'

'Okay, I promise.'

Johnny began to speak and Penny dutifully wrote down the words, hardly able to keep up with the fresh, clear, fully-formed copy that poured from him.

CLIENT: LIFEGEN

TITLE: NEAR DEATH

SFX: Black fills the screen and holds for
               several seconds — at least until the
               viewer begins to feel uncomfortable.
               A faltering heart beat booms in the
               dark and then stops. A bright light
               fills the screen and we see the figure
               of a man in a suit crumpled at his
               desk, in his hand a pen poised in the
               middle of signing an important
               document. The spirit of the same man
               leaves the body and shuffles towards
               the light. The man approaches the
               light and stops as he hears a great
               booming voice.

VOICE: Well? What do have to say for
               yourself?

MAN: (squinting into the light) I have
               worked hard. I have tried to be a
               good person.

153

VOICE: Yes, but haven't you forgotten
            something?

MAN: (uneasy) Well. There was that time
            that I overcharged a client but
            he . . .

VOICE: No. I mean haven't you forgotten
            something important?

MAN: (looking increasingly uneasy) Uh.
            Maybe I could have spent more time at
            home.

VOICE: True, but that's not what I had in
            mind.

MAN: Given more to charity?

VOICE: For heaven's sake, man. LifeGen. Did
            you talk to LifeGen?

MAN: (shaking his head in despair) Oh.
            No. I didn't . . .

VOICE: Didn't believe in Life Assurance?
            No. Most people don't until they get
            to this point.

MAN: (pale with fear and shaking his
            head) What does this mean?

            There is a long silence.

VOICE: It means that I am going to send you
            back. I'm going to give you another
            chance at life.

MAN: (clasping his hands together) Thank
                you. Thank you.

VOICE: But you must promise me one thing.

MAN: Anything. Anything.

VOICE: Those unbelievers. Tell them to talk
                to LifeGen.

MAN: (bowing and genuflecting and
                retreating) I promise. Yes. Yes.
                Thank you.

VOICE-OVER: For life after death, talk to
                LifeGen.

TWENTY-FOUR

On the Sunday, as Johnny waited for the doctor to dismiss him from the hospital, a priest entered the ward. He was hard to ignore: even stooped he was six feet four; he wore a black cassock and an eyepatch and moved from bed to bed talking in low tones. When the man loomed towards him and held out his hand, Johnny could feel himself preparing prickly, obnoxious sentences to send him away with.

'Can't shake,' Johnny said, holding up the valid excuse of his still-bandaged right hand while keeping his left resting upon his belly beneath the sheet.

'What happened?' the priest asked.

The truth seemed good enough.

'I cut it trying to break into a church.'

The priest wasn't discouraged.

'Why were you trying to break into a church?'

'I was looking for Jesus.'

The priest smiled.

'And did you find Him?'

Johnny shook his head.

The one eye narrowed. 'Are you still looking for Him?'

'No need.'

The priest kept his good eye friendly. 'Why not?'

Johnny shifted his position in the bed, his former calm ruffled.

His arm was beginning to itch but he didn't scratch it, he clasped his elbows and stared directly back at the one-eyed peddler of mendacity and protected himself from catching that disease of religion again.

'I don't believe in him.'

'That must be because you haven't met him,' the priest replied.

Very clever. Soften me up with your friendly intro and then smack me in the underbelly with that. Not so fast Your Priestliness. Don't think you've found a potential convert here. Don't think you can prey on me and pray over me while I'm down. That's why you're here, isn't it? To prey on the weak, the scared, the lonely. Selling your cheap wares is easy here. This lot are easy prey. I'm not buying your product. In the same way that I'm not buying a product that I know will fall apart the minute I leave the shop, I'm not buying your wares. You can tempt me with eternal life, mansions, an end to pain for ever; you can threaten me with everlasting hell, but when all is said and done I'm not buying it, not from you, not from anyone, not from Jesus himself – wherever He is. I'm sure there's a market out there – there's one right here, sitting captive. But I'm not a customer.

'I feel quite all right without Him. In fact, I have never felt better,' Johnny said.

Johnny kept looking at the eyepatch and at the priest's scar that ran above and below it in a diagonal from temple to cheek. 'What happened to your eye?' he asked.

The priest touched the patch in reflex. 'I lost it in a car crash.'

Johnny wanted to lift up that patch and look into the dead socket of nothingness and tell this priest that death was as dark and dud as that dead hole where there once was life. He was determined to stare down the one eye looking at him. The priest held his gaze, maintaining his fragile but insistent faith.

'What led you to look for Jesus in the first place?' he asked.

'Look, I know you've got a job to do, but I really

don't think it's for me. It's got me into too much trouble already. Don't feel sorry for me, Reverend. I am fine. I just want to get on with this life.'

'Well, I am holding a communion service in the ward this evening. You are still welcome to attend. Perhaps you will find what you haven't found.'

Is he deaf as well as half-blind?

'No thank you. I'm actually leaving the hospital this evening. Man doesn't live on bread wafers, he lives on a whole lot more than that. He needs money and houses and three meals a day.'

The chaplain seemed to find this amusing. He stood and continued to look full of hope for Johnny's soul, even though Johnny would gladly deny that he even had a soul to have hope for.

'I will pray for you,' he said.

'Feel free,' Johnny said and he watched the priest move on to easier targets – the old men in the ward who had less of life to love than he, and more reason to wish for something better. If he could have he would have offered them an alternative communion: a communion in celebration of this life. He would have liked to have broken bread with them: fresh bread, buttered and topped with smoked salmon and washed down with champagne so that they might all experience again what it is to feel a little living in this life.

TWENTY-FIVE

Johnny came back to life hardly believing he could have turned his back on something so lovely. He felt like a naive tourist, enthusiastic for even the least salubrious quarters of a second-rate city; able to find something exciting in the most mundane aspect.

It was summer and there was a lightness to people's movements, an ease of living and a taking of the pleasure life afforded them. And who could begrudge them this, he thought? Look at what they are enjoying: the sun, each other, the books they're reading, the restaurants, their cars, the music in their cars. Everywhere he looked there were men and women enjoying these things – now. And why? Because all of them were keeping busily focused on living. They were making the most of it. And that was the thing to do.

Walking to WWW Johnny began to imagine his reception back at the office. Would they notice a difference (beyond the scar and the haircut) in him? Would they see evidence of a change in his bearing. Would they envy him his steady calm and clarity, see the difference between Old Johnny Yells and New, Improved Johnny Yells?

Here at WWW we like to take a good long look at our staff and ask ourselves a very simple question. Can we improve them? And the answer is always – even with our most successful performers – yes.

In our effort to give you the very best we have to be perfectionists, and sometimes that means taking a long hard look at ourselves. At what we do.

It's this close scrutiny and attention to detail that keeps us ahead of our rivals. It's this unflinching drive to look at new ways of improving our staff, of eradicating weaknesses, that keeps us ahead of the field.

And it's this approach that has enabled us to bring you 'New, Improved Johnny Yells.'

At first glance he may just seem like the same old Johnny Yells that you know and love: the slim athletic build, the engaging brown eyes, the charm, the enthusiasm. He's still a winner of a Golden Plaque, creator of the most memorable campaign of the year, a diligent committed worker, fit, young and cost-effective.

But take a closer look and you'll begin to see the real change. We think you'll see a Johnny Yells that no longer gets distracted by the supposed big questions; a Johnny Yells that sleeps well at night without dreaming those restless troubling dreams; a Johnny Yells that feels healthy and happy; a Johnny Yells living in some style and comfort in the West of the city; a Johnny Yells that is free of the destructive metaphysical speculation that threatened to ruin his life; a Johnny Yells that doesn't see things that are not there; a Johnny Yells who won't let you down; a Johnny Yells that is better than ever before.

It wasn't easy. These improvements haven't just 'come about' by giving him a new haircut and a holiday. They are the result of weeks of intense and sometimes very difficult testing, pushing him to the very limit of his capacity. Many undergo these tests but few show the character, commitment and will required to pass.

New, Improved Johnny Yells has passed the test.

Of course, you don't have to take our word for it. Why don't you take a look for yourself? We think you'll like what you see.

New, Improved Johnny Yells. The change is for good.

He entered the Creative Department carefully, alert to any changes that might have taken place in the office: new faces, moved furniture. His own desk, he was relieved to see, had been left as it had been; there were

160

a number of yellow stickers noting calls taken, and a memo which he was about to read when a small crowd began to gather around his desk: Judy, Taylor, Bill.

'Aren't you going to tell us what happened, then?' Bill eventually asked. 'We've heard all kinds of stories. Judy said you almost died.'

'I did,' he said.

This drew an impressed silence. His colleagues all looked at him with concern, suddenly treating him with the eggshell respect afforded war veterans returning from conflict. They could see the scar on his arm, tantalizing evidence of something terrible.

He was glad that the details of his 'accident' remained obscure. He did not like to think of what these people would think of him if they really knew. Better to keep things vague and impressively mysterious.

'So what happened?' Bill asked.

'A freak accident in the house. I fell and knocked myself out and nearly bled to death in the process.'

'Well you look pretty good on it,' Judy said.

'Yeah, for someone who has been in hospital you look pretty good.'

'Thank you, Bill.'

'There's plenty to do,' Bill said. 'You should probably read that for a start.' He pointed to the memo. 'Your commercial has been approved. It was very nice. They want it shot right away and apparently they want another. You've done it.' Bill was unusually deferential, almost resigned.

'We should leave you to find your feet,' Judy said, shooing everyone away. She then drew in close by so that Bill and Taylor couldn't hear. 'W would like to have a chat with you when you've settled in,' she said.

Johnny could see Wollard at his desk, telephone inevitably in hand. His boss acknowledged him through the glass and Johnny watched and waited until Wollard had finished the call before walking into the inner sanctum, confidently. He realized, even as he was doing it, that he was the only one in the office who could have done such a thing: just strolled into Wollard's room like that, without knocking; but even while on the phone, Wollard had been watching him and waiting for him all this time.

Johnny wasn't one of the little fish on the mantelpiece any more; he was more like a remora that attaches itself to a shark and rides with the big fish in a symbiotic relationship. He didn't fully comprehend this, it didn't even need to be said, he just felt it: there was some silent understanding between them; a mutual appreciation and like-mindedness. Wollard's way was his way now.

Wollard spoke in a low, almost intimate tone. 'I'm glad that you haven't left us just yet. Your girlfriend said that you nearly died – is this true?'

Johnny nodded.

'It is.'

'Then you must feel happy to be alive.'

Despite the ever-present sardonic tone, Johnny thought his boss was quite serious in his questioning. Wollard, he noted, looked to be as old as the age he had managed to keep a secret; there were traces of silver in the slicked-back hair. His eyes were a little red-rimmed too. Was he finally beginning to fade?

'Your LifeGen commercial is a remarkable effort. The best script I've seen. They were a little nervous at first. But I reminded them that they wanted a frank and honest approach and a frank and honest approach is what you've given them. They want another – in a similar vein. Something that addresses the issue of death again. The sense of leaving it too late. That is precisely the route they want to go. Fear. It never fails. I trust you want to write the follow-up.'

Wollard looked out into the office.

'Your partner is a little disappointed. His own ideas were not as brilliant as he believed they were.'

From the bubble of Wollard's office it was still possible

162

to see the whole department and the whole department could see in. Bill's desk was in direct line of vision and he was looking in suspiciously, watching the interview.

'Let us go up to the Roof Terrace,' Wollard said. 'I have a proposition to make. I have to make a call first; I'll meet you there in five minutes.'

Johnny went back to his desk and found Bill following him.

'What was that all about, then?'

'Just a welcome back,' Johnny said. Bill, he now noted, was quieter, less sure of himself than usual: a fatal weakness.

In the lift to the top of the WWW Building, Johnny met the Director and owner of the agency, Mr Foster. Until now, Mr Foster had been a name and a photograph in advertising journals. In the flesh, he was a small, disappointing-looking man with a strange skin condition and a curiously cheap-looking suit.

'Johnny Yells?' Johnny was amazed that Mr Foster recognized him.

'Mr Foster.'

'LifeGen, right?'

'Right.'

'Good work. Keep it up. W tells me good things. Good things.'

Foster left the elevator at level eight leaving Johnny to proceed to ten with a pleasant glow.

Access to the Roof Terrace was exclusive to the Board Members; it was the first time that Johnny had been invited to the top and he was taken with the ambience. All manner of foliage and flowers crammed the space, except for a raised gazebo-like structure in the centre that afforded a three-hundred-and-sixty-degree view of the entire city.

When Wollard arrived he seemed to have regained something of the manic zing that marked him out from mere mortals. He clamped his arm upon Johnny's shoulder and steered him into the gazebo from where he proceeded to pick out the various landmarks and buildings in the city, giving a little architectural résumé of each. He showed his favourite running routes and Johnny began to wonder what this was all leading to, knowing full well that it was leading to something. He felt, looking at the city like this, that Wollard was about to offer him the earth.

'I have been following your progress this last year, very carefully. You have come on. There are good creatives everywhere, plenty of them. People with ideas, people who love words, who have a facility to manipulate them into telling phrases; people who know exactly what image is right for what product. But more often than not, they lack the special ruthlessness to carry it all through: they become lazy, they become distracted.'

He leant in a little like a father imparting wisdom to a son, telling him the secrets of life. 'Business is a game, and like a game it requires skilful athletes who are dedicated and single-minded; it requires an indifference to emotional distraction, to weakness, frailty; a refusal to let life get in the way of a good idea. Faxing your script from your sickbed showed that. I have noted these qualities in you. And that is why I would like you to be my Creative Director.'

Given his age, his experience and his recent difficulties, it was an unexpected offer.

'What . . . about you?' Johnny asked, tactfully.

'I will be a kind of Executive Creative Director. I need more time to pursue my hobbies. My little gallery is ready to be opened to the public very soon and it will require my presence. You don't have to give me an answer now. Think about it for a few days, but think about it amongst yourself.'

Johnny looked at the city lying before him, tracing the running path that Wollard had shown him. He then looked over west to his new neighbourhood, a distance of some four miles from here. It was, he thought, an ideal distance for a young Creative Director to run every day, especially one determined to remain fitter than any in the company.

TWENTY-SIX

The collateral of promotion put Johnny in a mood to spend. 'I need some new boots,' he said to Penny as he cooked their breakfast, the last breakfast he would cook and eat in rented accommodation. 'I know the ones I want.'

He had decided that he was going to get them. A Creative Director had a certain sartorial responsibility. Look at Wollard. Didn't his apparel proclaim him? His clothes were made to measure his every achievement, each square inch of fabric was a little monument to some victory. Johnny should emulate that, start to cut his own dash. He would begin from the ground up with those boots.

'We can go for a drive around the city and then go to some shops, buy some new clothes, eat lunch and then go to the film,' he said.

Johnny enjoyed the compartmentalized pleasure of the new car, with its comforts and securities, and all those dials telling him what was what. If there was a dial capable of measuring his contentment now it would give a high reading. If ten was total satisfaction then he was an eight rising to a nine. Looking at the faces of the people shopping and driving, he felt that most people existed at a steady five, often never rising above even that. At least he had a chance to help them push up their scores by cheering them with the promise of life-enhancing, image-improving, happiness-serving products. As he drove he offered up a silent prayer of thanks to whatever it was that had brought him to this moment now in such fine fettle. It wasn't an intimate prayer to a known being; it was just a general thank you to the empty air or to chance or to whatever apparatus was responsible for the confluence of pleasing circumstances in his life.

How delicious it was to feel the shop assistant lower the foot-bar to his foot and the tape measure about his instep, and then to smell the leather of the boots as they crinkled out of the tissue paper. He took his time lacing one while the assistant laced the other.

The advertisement for these boots claimed that they would last for thirty years, longer than a job, longer than a marriage, longer than some people lived.

'*Boots for Life*,' Johnny said, enunciating the Grantly Grants motto.

'They will certainly last a lifetime if they're properly cared for, sir,' the shop assistant said.

'How long might that be?' Johnny asked the assistant, a perfectly groomed man with a tape measure about his neck and a suit from another era. The man looked at Johnny as if able to predict the length of his life.

'In your case, sir, I would say at least fifty years.'

Fifty years. Half a century. Some way into the next century. Nearly twice what he had already lived. Johnny knew this to be the simple flattery of a good salesman but he hoped it were true.

'I'll settle for that,' he said. 'But if I fall short I'd like my money back.'

The assistant said he'd make sure madam was fully recompensed. Johnny slipped on the boots that might outlive him.

'Why don't you walk up and down in them, sir?'

Johnny did this, watched by the assistant and Penny. Already he could feel the assurance surging up from his feet, instilling him with a swagger. The new leather was firm against his instep, but the fit was perfect. The quality could not be denied.

'I'm not just saying this, but they really do become you, sir,' the assistant said as Johnny walked up and down the length of the shop. 'They seem to give you belief in yourself.'

Johnny didn't doubt it; he knew of the ability of mere things to have such power; it was part of his job to invest inanimate objects with human characteristics: happy tomatoes, thoughtful kettles, elitist marmalades.

'I'll take them, and keep them on. You can throw the old ones.'

The assistant took away the old shoes, pinching them between thumb and forefinger. Johnny had shed his tawdry old skin and was emerging in a far tougher and classier covering.

The shop assistant had not been lying: outside, Johnny did feel different about himself in these boots, as if they had refined him in some way.

'How are they?' Penny asked.

He thought about it. 'Snug.'

They started back through the arcade and the criss-crossing shoppers. As they passed a fountain in the centre of the plaza Penny pointed to someone in the crowd: a street artist drawing portraits.

'Isn't that your friend, the one you used to work with? What's his name?'

Johnny could see him and he turned his face slightly sideways hoping that he had not been seen.

Edson was sitting on a short stool, leaning forward to sketch a portrait of a young woman. Johnny's heartbeat, steady and untroubled for many weeks now, began to percuss powerfully.

'How funny,' Johnny said.

'Aren't you going to say hello?'

'What about the meter?'

'We've got time.'

They walked over and stood a little behind Edson so as to watch him sketch. The drawing was nearly done. Edson's great talent for finding a likeness had not diminished; with a few simple lines he was able to get the essence of the girl, each little pencil stroke making the face truer. When he was done, he signed his name in the corner, dated it and turned it for the sitter to see.

The girl was at best plain and many a street sketcher would have made a lift here, a tuck there, lengthened the eyelashes a little; but Edson had avoided flattery, going instead for what was true and in doing so he caught her exactly. She looked pleased with the drawing, but the boyfriend seemed unconvinced. Perhaps he believed his girlfriend to be more beautiful than this.

'I like it,' she said. 'It's good. Charlie? What do you think?'

'It makes you look a bit serious,' he said. 'How much?'

'Whatever you want to pay,' Edson said, his business sense still abject, Johnny noted.

'Will ten do?' the young man asked, taking advantage.

'Fine,' Edson said.

'I'd say it's worth twenty,' Johnny said.

The three all turned to look at him, the girl with agreement in her face, the boyfriend with suspicion, and Edson with happy surprise. 'Johnny Yells,' he said, and he stood up to embrace him. Johnny put out his good hand so that he might shake rather than hug.

'I don't mind paying twenty,' the girl said.

'He said ten was okay,' the young man protested.

'Why not meet halfway,' Johnny suggested.

Edson shrugged, happy, no doubt, to draw it for nothing.

'Who are you – his agent or something?' the young man asked Johnny, getting aggressive.

'Give him fifteen, Charlie. It's a good drawing,' the girl said.

The truculent young man reached for the fifteen

pounds, counted it out heavily, and handed it to Edson. He then left with his immortalized girl who smiled apologetically for her partner's mean-spiritedness.

'Thank you,' Edson said to Johnny. 'Perhaps you *should* be my agent.'

'You remember Penny?' Johnny asked.

'Yes.' Edson and Penny shook hands.

'That was a great drawing,' Penny said. 'You had her just right. That's a talent you have.'

'It's got him into trouble in the past, hey, Eddy?'

'Why don't you let him draw you, J?' Penny suggested. 'We're going to need some pictures for the house. I can go and get some things while he does you.'

Johnny didn't like the idea of being left alone with Edson but he reminded himself that he had nothing to fear and that Edson probably needed the money. He shrugged and sat in the model's chair. 'I'll be here,' he said to Penny who headed off through the crowds.

Johnny fidgeted in his seat. He was nervous, the same way he felt in a dentist's chair, anticipating extractions.

'It's good to see you, Johnny Yells. I've been thinking about you a lot since that time you called,' Edson said, sharpening a pencil with a razor. 'I called you back a few times but failed to get you. You sounded like you were in bad shape. What was it?'

'Oh, that! I was being an idiot. I was drunk and thought I'd ring you for a laugh. It was nothing. I was out of my head. I should have rung you back to apologize.'

'Okay, look at me,' Edson said, gentle and firm.

Johnny looked at Edson but avoided looking at those eyes, focusing instead on his nose.

'So, you have found your vocation.'

'It's a little pocket money. Hold still.'

The scar on Johnny's arm was suddenly itching, almost burning. He tried to remain still for the pose and disguise his discomfort.

'Can you look at me straight – I need to see your eyes.

170

Up a bit, that's it. You look slimmer – maybe it's the haircut.'

'I have been keeping fit.'

'Still going to that club?'

'Yep. Still living in Downs?'

'Still there.'

With such poor aspirations, you'll live there for ever.

Johnny wondered if Edson's material disinterest would hold up when faced with the enviable structures of another man's success.

'I'm finally moving to Park West Gardens. We've bought a flat.'

'You've got what you wanted?' Edson asked, no hint of anything that might be called envy in his voice.

'Remember that flat I told you about, months ago? The one with a view of Wollard's house? It's that one. So what are you doing besides this?'

'Teaching art – at The Centre.'

'I can see you as a teacher,' Johnny said.

'Look up again. You keep dropping your head.'

Looking at Edson was like looking at some mirror that showed Johnny at his worst. To counter this feeling Johnny tried to drum up the faith in life he had recently found, the assurance he had gained; but it remained vague, like an illusion. He moved his toes about in the new boots searching for it there.

'You must have been pleased to see your own ads all over the city,' Edson said. 'Every time I saw a LifeGen poster I thought of you.'

'I must have been constantly on your mind then,' Johnny said.

The itch was unbearable now and he started to scratch it by the wrist where it was possible to see the jagged gash scar. How Edson would love to know of the trauma Johnny had gone through. If only he knew how close Johnny had been to blurting it all out that night. What would he have made of it? No doubt he would have told

Johnny that it was a sign of some kind. Perhaps he might have said that it was God speaking to him, trying to get his attention.

Edson was screwing up his face to get some detail exact; every time he looked down at his pad, Johnny rubbed his wrist, keeping the scar turned away from view.

When finally Edson held up his pad and turned it round Johnny saw, staring back at him, a serious, troubled Johnny Yells, a Johnny Yells he thought he had left behind.

Edson had brought to the surface all the inner squirming and turmoil that Johnny had tried to disguise. The eyes looked shiftily askance, the jaw grimaced. The hair – which was slicked back with the gel that Wollard had recommended he buy from Frundy's – was tight on his scalp; the mouth had a sardonic snarl. All the nuances of his inner self were turned outward and exposed by this x-ray talent. His soul – if he had a soul – was lain bare there on the paper. It was him all right – a subterranean version of him, caught in the light of Edson's brilliance.

Johnny knew that Edson had him.

Penny arrived with more carrier bags. Johnny, who had not responded to the drawing yet, turned it for her to see.

'What do you think?'

'Well. You've got something. It's very good. It's very good. It's really distinguished,' she said, pedalling back from her initial reaction. 'Do you like it?'

'Is that how you see me, Eddy?' Johnny asked.

'At the moment, it is.'

Maybe he was just imagining things again; perhaps it was unwitting, just a consistency of style. It could be the gel. Or perhaps it was just his conscience. Whatever it was, the portrait reminded Johnny of the seditious sketch that had cost Edson his job; the similarity was uncanny; Edson couldn't have been innocent of that. But then it was probably just Johnny's foolish guilt that made him see it this way. He said nothing of it.

Another eager shopper was waiting to have her portrait done. 'Don't let me deprive you of work,' Johnny said, stepping aside. 'Twenty?'

'No. Take it. On the house. You've already doubled my wages.'

'Don't be silly.'

'I insist.'

'Well, I'm glad we bumped into each other,' Johnny said. 'Maybe I'll give you a call. A sober call this time. I've got your number,' Johnny said, not wanting to see Edson again. Ever. They shook hands, and Edson held his hand for a second and looked down at it.

'What happened to you?'

The scar was red from the rubbing.

DIY,' Johnny said. 'One of the many hazards of buying your own home.'

He knew that Edson knew he was lying; and he could have told him the truth, he had nothing to fear from that. But there wasn't time to go into it now, not here. And there never would be time because he wouldn't see Edson unless some trick of happenstance threw them together again; they were on diverging roads, travelling at different speeds and the roads were unlikely ever to intersect again.

'I'll call you,' Johnny lied again, keen to get moving before Penny invited Edson to their house-warming party. When he had walked a fair distance he looked back and Edson was still looking at him, as if expecting Johnny to turn.

TWENTY-SEVEN

In his own home, Johnny tried to enjoy and distil the sense of ownership and suppress the thought he had had for most of the day, which was just how quickly a dream realized turned so blandly into a matter of fact. He walked from room to room trying to remind himself of the initial delight he had experienced upon walking through these rooms, and of what it meant to live here, in Park West Gardens, in the very flat he had wanted; but that feeling remained elusive, like a sneeze not happening. Was he imagining it, or was this flat smaller than it looked that first day he saw it?

While Penny hung pictures and designated homes for things with a tireless delight he tried to rekindle his enthusiasm, stave off his creeping disappointment by asking her what went where. 'What about this?' he asked, holding up a lamp.

She pointed him straight away to a place she had already assigned.

'And this. What is this?' He lifted a small sculpture of a man's torso.

'It's a sculpture. I thought that could go in our room.'

'I'm not sure I want to wake up to this.'

'Well, put it there for the minute.'

Penny had a lot of stuff: clothes, shoes, pictures, books, artefacts – stuff. And all this stuff was diminishing the space.

'How long is this room meant to be?' he asked Penny

174

of the living room, puzzling at the floor and measuring it out.

'It looks smaller because of all the boxes,' Penny said.

Of course, once everything was packed away and in its place, the flat would look bigger. It was a fair space, much bigger than the space in which he had lived before. He pushed the boxes to the side to clear some more room.

'Johnny?' Penny had her hands out in question.

'Just want to see what it's like without the clutter. That's a bit better.'

'You could put the boxes in the tip. Why not make a little bonfire? There's so much rubbish.'

He moved aside another heavier box.

'What's in here?' he asked, peeling newspaper away to see what was contained in the box.

'It's a dinner service. Johnny, are you going to question everything?'

'Where are we going to put it?'

'I don't know. Look. Why don't you do something useful? Throw these boxes.'

He began to gather them, fold them and slide them one into the other.

'We should keep them,' he said.

'Keep them?'

'We may move again some day. We might need them.'

'We won't be moving for a long time.'

'I'll put them in the store cupboard.'

All this unpacking and reaching and lifting was troubling his arm, which every time it itched and burnt reminded him of other trouble. He dragged the boxes to the store cupboard, reassured by the thought of having them ready to pack to move to a larger home one day.

He lifted the trap door and fiddled in the dark for the light switch. He pushed the boxes into the corner ahead where the bare light bulb threw its glare and he noticed the flicker of moths. He watched them dance about the light as though it were the only thing they had to live for; he marvelled at the simple satisfactions and the short life of a moth, which waits for the once-in-a-lifetime flicking on of a switch to brighten its existence.

New niggles trailed him through the new house, popping up in cupboards that seemed smaller than he remembered and in fixtures and fittings that lost their appeal now that he owned them. He grew irritated with himself for his lack of gratitude. Why was he so quickly unsatisfied with what he thought would satisfy? Exactly how large did these rooms have to be for his desire to be placated?

It's tiredness and excitement and the mundanity of moving in. You'll begin to appreciate it when you're settled.

He knew that there were still elements of his old self that would take time to eradicate, and that some of those traits would surface from time to time like a low-lying virus. But at what point exactly could he feel settled, when in this life would he feel some permanent sense of well-being? Did it have to remain a little ahead of him in the guise of something not yet owned or achieved? Damn it! Wasn't his recent experience, his near-death, enough to make him appreciate things a little more than he did now? Where was 'New, Improved Johnny Yells', and his New, Improved attitude?

When he returned to the living room Penny was attending to the detail of hanging pictures and photographs.

'You could put these on the mantelpiece,' she said, passing him some small photographs in silver frames – one of them together, one of Penny skiing, one of him sitting at the table with his Golden Plaque, taken just after receiving the award. In it he looked pale and bewildered. He stood the pictures on the ledge, either side of the impressive, embossed and gilt-rimmed invitation to Wollard's birthday celebration.

'What shall we do with this?' Penny asked, unrolling and holding up Edson's portrait of Johnny. Johnny looked at it. It was a fine picture still, good enough to frame and hang. But it wasn't a Johnny Yells he wanted to advertise.

'Put it in the case,' he said, indicating the deep, leather suitcase in which he collected things he could not quite throw away.

'Good. I never liked it.' Penny folded the portrait and put it in the case, pausing to look at what was in it. The little brown bag with the Bible was there, at the top.

'Are you going to keep all this stuff?'

'I'll sort it later,' he said. He would get rid of the things in that case very soon. Perhaps tomorrow he would build a bonfire. He went and closed the incriminating suitcase and put it to one side.

'I'd better fix the punch. Are we done?'

He went to get the ice bags and fruit for the punch and took it to the garden where he began to mix the drink, mixing it strongly. He tasted it and the vague unease that had accompanied him all day was countered by the cocktail's kick and the sudden thought of his friends arriving at his house and seeing it for the first time and the open admiration they would express and the hidden envy they would feel for his place and, by extension, him.

He checked his watch again. The fluorescent dots on the hour and minute hands were coming to life as the late summer light faded and the streetlights began to illume the hazy dusk.

Later, when the guests arrived, Johnny's faith in life was temporarily restored by the effusive praise heaped upon him, Penny, their beautiful home; car, clothes, haircut, promotion and general well-being. The easy compliments and their half-truths were like quick-acting medication staving off the pain for a while.

But the near perfection of his circumstances and the

acknowledgement of this could not stop the restless troubling inside, eating him like a rust, discolouring the bright shininess of his life. He found himself avoiding conversation, using the escape of serving drinks to keep him on the move, just ahead of the stalking reproach that was after him again. The dread that he thought he had buried back there with his breakdown was surfacing at a most inopportune time. He took a deep, disciplined breath and went out to the garden.

A lone figure crouched beneath the tree. It was Albert and he was smoking. Johnny went and knelt down to join his friend.

'Can I have some of that?'

A silent Albert drew a curly wisp of smoke from his mouth and handed the smoke to Johnny who drew in a breath so long that there was no smoke for a while. He exhaled and waited for the narcotic's deadening happiness to have a long, nice talk with his anxious heart, to settle it and blank this spreading fear.

'This is a fine place,' Albert said, his features hidden in a dark, black cloud, his voice lowered for intimate discussion.

Johnny sucked in again and leaned against the tree, looking round to make sure of their privacy. For a time he forgot what it was that had been troubling him. They looked up at the stars and at the lights, up towards the crest where The Mansions twinkled. Behind them, the music throbbed and the laughter became more abandoned.

'You seem well,' Albert said.

'I am,' Johnny said, believing it again. The dead blanketing of the drug was calming his nerves.

Johnny could feel the curling question mark on Albert's list lifting away from the J.

'No question marks over me now?'

'I had my worries about you, I must confess. For a while I thought that you were going to succumb to religion. When you started asking me those questions about death, when you were ill, I really thought you were ripe for it. But you've come through your crisis valiantly.'

'It hardly seems like me – back then,' Johnny said.

'We all go through it. It's just that some go through it and don't come out the other side. They get caught thinking they have an answer. They won't accept that there is nothing, so they make up something.'

Albert took back the smoke and inhaled deeply. In this little discussion Johnny thought he could detect Albert's own fears.

Penny stumbled from the door and slouched up against the car, parked high up the drive. She began to laugh, pointing at them, finding something hilarious.

'I thought you were . . . I thought . . .' She flopped and swayed like a spineless ballerina. She collapsed beneath the weight of her own joke, weak with laughter and wine.

Bill then appeared, drunk too. He hailed the neighbourhood. 'Nice car, Johnny. I peed on it. Don't worry. Won't corrode for years. Hey. Why don't you take us round the block? I can pretend I'm a Creative Director for a few minutes. Ha! Just kidding.'

'Yes. Why don't we go for a spin?' Johnny said.

'Fine motor,' Albert said.

The car – part of Johnny's promotional package – was in shadow but there was sufficient light to accentuate the low-slung features and the moody power.

The Shapiro GT Convertible. It's a hell of a drive.

This was the car that Wollard had, in last year's most expensive shoot, sent through hoops of fire, around barrels of burning sulphur to a full orchestral soundtrack, while the Four Horsemen of the Apocalypse rode hot behind.

Johnny stood up and walked towards it. He stroked it for solace. It was all his. He opened the door.

'You can't drive, if you're drunk,' Penny said.

He wasn't drunk, he was as sober as death.

'Who's coming? Are you coming?'

'Pull the roof down,' Bill said. He got in the passenger seat. Albert followed, dextrously holding wine glass, joint and bottle. Johnny flipped the driver's seat forward and Albert squeaked into the leather bucket seat behind.

'Pen?'

'Boys' toys.'

Johnny got in and started the car and watched the dials light up. He pulled the roof back and pushed the tape in: Great Music from Great Commercials, Volume II. It was already rewound to the right place. He waited for the slow bubbling thunder of voices chanting in staccato unison and then the double basses underpinning it with a sinister organic throb.

'Wayhay!' Bill shouted.

Johnny could hear the hooves of the four riders galloping over the booming bass and in the rear mirror he could see the reds of their eyes and the snort of their reinless, feral steeds. He jerked the car in a violin squeal of rubber from the drive, accelerating to the first sleeping policeman and leaving the ground over it.

'Fine acceleration,' Albert said, attempting to put on his seat belt.

'Where are we going then?' Bill asked.

'Not so fast, Johnny,' Albert said.

Johnny moved up through the gears, keeping the power in check. The truth of a car like this could not be experienced on these roads, at this speed, he thought.

He took them out of Park West Gardens' serene streets, out onto the Western Highway where the open road widened to three lanes and would be as clear as a runway.

'Where are we going?' Albert asked.

At the entrance to the Highway Johnny put his foot down and they were all pushed back into their seats, the car keeping just ahead of the bright ball of fire in his mind, and the ghoulish riders, especially Mr Death at the head of the posse.

'Steady, Johnny,' Albert said, shouting above the wind.

Into overdrive, the revolutions dropping from the red.

'What are you afraid of?' Johnny asked Albert, his hands like clamps on the wheel, his eyes darting from the road to the mirror where on the back seat Albert sat at an angle. He had thrown the joint and put down the wine and his arms hugged his knees in a crash position.

'Breaking the law,' he said.

'It's the only way you can experience the Shapiro's power. Ha! Ha! Ha!' Bill screamed.

Johnny flipped the switch and a rush of extra speed deafened him and muffled whatever it was Albert was trying to say. The road came at them like a curving torch-light procession. There was nothing in front or behind them except the ghouls.

The roads were eerily clear, just the lights of houses flickered behind them.

'You need to get to 130 for the double turbo to kick in!' Bill screamed.

The needles were nearly all at maximum.

With the Shapiro there's no safer way to feel the thrill of danger.

'Johnny, seriously.' Albert was leaning forward, shouting into his ear. 'I feel uneasy going this fast.'

A car appeared ahead and they were past it as though it were standing still.

'Slow, please.'

The orange glow of the distant city began to recede as the Shapiro delivered its credential top speed of 150.

'Please, Jesus.'

'There's nothing to fear,' Johnny yelled. 'The Shapiro's handling is second to none. Even if I suddenly move the steering wheel – like this – nothing will happen. The faster the steadier.'

In the mirror, Albert dipped out of view.

Johnny drove on at full tilt and remembered that there was nothing to fear, even if he died now. Then, having reminded himself of this, he eased down. He had out-driven death and his cohorts. The thrill of riding the thin divide had made him feel glad to be alive again.

He pulled over and turned back to the city, happy that he had stolen sufficient lead over his pursuers, for a while. In the back Albert sat well forward with his head in his lap, praying for his life, clinging to it, the way Johnny suspected he would.

CLIENT: LIFEGEN

TITLE: FUNERAL

SFX: We move above ground level over
             trees and fields towards a lone
             church where a black-clad crowd
             stands huddled around a grave. We
             close-up on the face of the priest
             conducting the funeral rites. He is
             solemn and looking skyward. Music —
             a sonorous funeral plod — fades in
             over the scene and the priest begins
             the ceremony. We pan around the
             group of grief-stricken relatives
             dabbing handkerchiefs and sniffling.
             One or two maintain a grim-faced
             stiffness. The camera closes in on a
             young man who appears to be watching
             the scene, when he turns to the
             camera and starts to talk in a
             respectful whisper as the music
             lowers but continues.

YOUNG MAN: Death. It's not something we like to
             face. The trouble is, it's always the
             ones left behind who have to face it.
             (close-up on crying woman) That's the
             widow. It was quite a shock when
             George, her husband, died. He seemed
             to be in reasonably good health. A
             little overweight perhaps, tended to
             work a little too hard. He dropped
             dead at his desk. Heart attack. He was
             fifty. (back to the grave)

VICAR: If only he'd talked to LifeGen.

183

GATHERING: If only he'd talked to LifeGen.
              (back to young man.)

YOUNG MAN: It's a common tragedy. Fifty per
              cent of men die before they reach the
              end of their working life. And half
              of them again have not made
              provision for the family that
              survives them.

VICAR: If only he'd talked to LifeGen.

GATHERING: If only he'd talked to LifeGen.

YOUNG MAN: And the main reason is that most
              people, men especially, simply will
              not contemplate the possibility of
              their own death. And by avoiding it
              they end up depriving others of the
              possibility of life. (we see the
              family) George believed in life
              after death but it isn't the kind
              that will take care of their
              financial needs now that he is gone.
              If he'd talked to LifeGen his family
              would now at least be financially
              secure.
                 If you don't like to think about
              death and haven't thought about life
              assurance yet, talk to LifeGen.
              We'll tell you all there is to know
              about life after death and put your
              fears at rest.

VOICE-OVER: For life after death, talk to
              LifeGen.

184

TWENTY-EIGHT

Johnny set off for The Mansions alone. Penny had been invited too, but she had a prior engagement and Johnny was glad of this: of late he had felt the entwining of their lives to be a strangulation; he had almost forgotten how wonderful the world could look to a man without ties.

The Mansions were at the highest elevation in the city, the walk from 29 Clamber Road to Wollard's house involving a steep climb. And as he climbed Johnny began to appreciate the change in the air. He saw why the rich favoured altitude. This air and these houses reminded him that he still had further to go in life in order to breathe the rarefied air up here instead of the comparatively fumy stifle of Park West Gardens. The houses he was walking by now, mystically in half-view at the end of long drives, were, without doubt, bigger, better, more comfortable and filled with finer quality furniture than his own home.

When he reached the top of the hill and stopped to admire the view he noted that he was breathing evenly and that he was not sweating from the climb. The work-out was paying dividends. He was glad of this for he did not want to soil his suit or grime up the white starched collar. He checked his watch and saw that he was early so he took a cigarette from his pocket and smoked, taking in the dizzy heights of possibility.

Up here it was possible to believe in a higher existence, one free of all worry. Even now, he felt as if he had risen to a new, refined state, a place above the scrabbling and grabbing that took place down there, in the city where men and women fought for their little plots and patches. These were the Mansions of heaven that he was looking for and there was no going back down the hill to a middling grind of minor aspiration now that he had seen them.

A car passed slowly and he saw the driver looking for an entrance. He stubbed out his cigarette and followed the sedan, brushing back his hair, checking his watch again without registering the time. The porterless gates opened and he passed into the grounds, the gates clanking closed behind. He walked up the gypsum drive half watching the trees for dogs. Some sweet smell came off those trees and there was a fiery glow of flickering lights seen through the tight leaves.

As the house came into view he paused to take in its extent. The house was gabled and Johnny saw straight away a W in the three V's of the roof. Closer scrutiny made it clear that the two outer v's had been left unpainted, leaving the black W prominent. It was as if Wollard was leaving little marks, some permanent record of himself wherever he could.

At the front door he was greeted by waiters dressed in white jackets, bearing silver trays laden with champagne. Johnny took a glass and walked into the hallway. His gaze was immediately drawn upwards to view the painting on the ceiling: a kind of astrological chart with stylized stars and planets and dotted lines linking them in patterns, and in the centre, in the recess of a dome, the sun, unrealistic but believable, radiating like a child's picture of a sunflower. The mural conveyed some secret order, some hidden connection between all things.

'Canapes, sir?'

He took a crab roulade and a devil-on-horseback and meandered between the smartly attired guests, looking for familiar faces. He recognized no-one yet. The style and sound of the gathering were distinctly refined, almost ornate, a far cry from the brash rabble Wollard presided over at WWW. Wollard had, it seemed, another life away from the cheap transience of advertising. He was collecting his art about him and mixing with people who might appreciate it. Johnny was getting a glimpse of the inner caucus of Wollard's world.

At the far end of the room he saw Wollard's sister, talking in a cursory way to an elderly gentleman. He remembered her from the Golden Plaque Awards Ceremony and as he approached her he was relieved and flattered to see that she remembered him.

'It's Diane, isn't it?'

'And you . . .'

'Johnny.'

'The award winner.'

They shook hands.

Looking at her Johnny could see the refinement of what in Wollard was a vague and ugly combination of features; in her they achieved a fine symmetry; only the hair had the exact likeness in colour and texture to that of her brother. She had a strong, equine beauty and skittish movements. Her dress was the colour of old blood and her hair had been coaxed and teased into snake ringlets. Her hands were gloved in ivory chamois and her jewellery was all red garnet, or perhaps ruby.

Johnny felt an immediate and barely disguised lust for her, a powerful excitement like the tingle of crossing borders into new, potentially rich, unclaimed territory.

'I was looking at the ceiling,' Johnny said. 'Wondering what it meant.'

'It's an astrolocart: a kind of map of the stars. My father had it done many years ago. People turn up from all over the country to see it. There is meant to be some code in it but I've never worked it out. Do you have a cigarette?'

He offered her one and lit it for her, the flame of his lighter set a little too high and wavering in the airy hall.

He tried hard not to brown her tip, wanting to preserve her perfection and her to think well of him.

'Your brother has an amazing place here.'

'Actually, it's the family home. Father's. But he is never here; he lives abroad. I live here most of the time.'

'So where does W live?'

'He has a house on Grand Avenue.'

Johnny's calculations and estimations of Wollard's wealth seemed suddenly puerile, like schoolboy guesses. While he had been saving pennies to buy a cardboard box everyone around him already had two palaces. He felt like a peon in the company of a princess.

'You live alone, here?'

'W stays here from time to time. He has the gallery to play with.'

Some cheers and whoops and clapping sounded and Wollard appeared, wearing a bright white linen suit of impeccable cut and credential; he clapped his hands and opened his arms, received greetings and congratulation and then proceeded to make a circuit of the room to much genuflecting and bowing from the guests. Although Johnny knew no-one in the room Wollard seemed to connect with everyone in some intimate way; he was the glue that bound them all, the spider conductor spinning his glistening thread. And when Wollard finally came to Johnny, and gave him a tactile two-handed shake and then placed a hand on his shoulder, Johnny felt that he was on one of those threads, walking its silky course into the web.

'My replacement,' Wollard said.

Although his normal manner was histrionic, Wollard was acting, playing a new role that Johnny was not used to seeing. His accent was more choice, his manner more affected.

'I see you've been talking to my curator,' he said. 'D, you should be very grateful to this young man. It is his talent that has freed me up to run the gallery. Perhaps

188

you'll give our guest a little private view later. There is something I would like him to see. You'll need a light. The power is down. And don't tell the others or they'll all want a peep.'

Someone pulled Wollard away to kiss and congratulate him and he spun away to embrace them.

'So you look after the paintings?' Johnny asked.

'W has impressionable taste. Too much money can blur discernment. Let's say I advise him.'

Johnny couldn't say for sure but something in her manner invited indiscretion.

'I should like to see the collection.'

A gong suddenly brought the room to silence and Wollard mounted the stairs halfway to address the room.

'Fifty years old,' he began.

Gasps and incredulous cries of 'Never.'

'It sounds like halfway but with the exception of the very lucky few, it's more realistically two thirds. In my effort to prolong the years I have searched high and low for an elixir, the one true immortal brew. If any of you have the secret then please see me afterwards. In the meantime I will be making the most of my last third. The Wollard Gallery – I couldn't get them to name the agency after me – will be opening very soon. We have a little lighting problem that has delayed things; but I expect to see you all here in a few weeks time. All of you in this room have contributed in some way to the collection and today's celebration is as much a thank you to you as it is a happy return for me. I thank you all for coming and sustaining me over the years. Here's to life, friends and art.'

'Life, friends and art,' the room repeated. There was then quiet as everyone drank to the host and gave thought to the words just spoken, then applause and a resuming of conversation.

A woman sidled up to Diane. 'So, tell me D, is it true that W put all the Friedmans in the collection?'

'You will have to wait and see, Molly. W is very secretive about what is and isn't to be included. He wants it all to be a surprise.'

'I hear that you have helped him.'

'He needs someone to tell him how good a painting really is.'

During this exchange, Johnny kept his eyes on Diane and thought it possible to see himself living with her in this house. Such a union was, as yet, all in his head, but it was not implausible and the attractiveness of this thought made it hard to concentrate on anything else. He drank more champagne to fortify the alchemy. He stared at the v at the nape of her neck where the snake ringlets bunched, wanting to run his finger there.

You can live here, Yells. This is your chance.

'Why don't you show me the house?' he said, cutting into her dialogue boldly.

She looked at him coolly.

'Do you want the short tour or the detailed tour?'

'The detailed.'

'If you'll excuse us, Molly?'

Diane directed him up the stairs and began to adopt the neutral, instructive tone of a tour guide.

'This is my father's study.'

He listened to her discourse on the swirling motifs, the magnificence of the bookcase packed with hardbound volumes on art, philosophy, astrology and theology. All the while she kept from meeting his eyes and kept a prim, straight back while discussing every artefact and object in agonizing detail.

'The books in this room comprise the finest private collection on astrology in the country. The silver belonged to my mother. This is an ink well.' She held up the shiny receptacle before him.

'Moving on to the guest room.'

Still the game of museum attendant and tourist; still

his dark fermenting lust and fanciful notion of living in these very rooms.

'This is W's room – when he stays.'

Wollard's room was a vast rectangle. At the foot of the bed there was a black soapstone bust of Wollard – flattered and lionized.

'The nose is wrong,' she said. Running her little finger along the bridge of the bust. 'We Wollards have a little bump.'

On into her room. Johnny nearly broke the game and ran his own little finger along the bridge of her nose to compare the line to feel for the little hereditary imperfection that should have been there in the sculpture of her brother; but she moved on with the tour, leading him back to the study to look for something in the bureau. She held up a large, archaic key. 'For the later stage of the tour.'

She led him from the room coaxing more facts from the furniture, pausing before 'one of the most valuable pieces in the house'. On the way down the stairs they met a guest about to use the bathroom.

'Diane,' he said, 'I haven't talked to you all night.'

She touched the side of the man's cheek. 'I'll come and find you, Stephen.' This seemed to appease the tipsy man, but it only served to increase the pain in Johnny's abdomen.

'Who is that?' he asked.

'Stephen Friedman.'

Johnny watched the artist stagger away and he reminded himself how little he had liked his paintings.

Diane led him through to the back of the house, out onto the veranda, into the cool evening. The sun was well down now and there was no trace of the orange in the sky; just the luminous glowing throb of the city's collective electricity, the individual dots of light cramming together like a badly planned heaven.

They paused to look at the lights.

'Where do *you* live?' she asked.

He looked over to the west, nearest the ridge.

'Just there.' Fine though the area was, he was embarrassed to name it.

She peered down towards Park West Gardens.

'We're neighbours.'

We could be so much more than that.

Over the lawn, a long stone building reflected the candlelight glow from the house.

'On to the most important part of the tour.'

They began to walk across the lawn and Johnny picked up the scent of passing summer and skidded slightly on the cut grass which stuck to the soles of his boots. He offered Diane his arm and she held it until they reached the door of the gallery.

'What about security?' he asked, as she put the single key in the door.

'The collection is uninsurable,' she said. 'We let the dogs out from time to time.' Johnny looked over into the trees, still wondering when the snapping dogs would come rushing to intercept them.

The door swung inwards and they were in a darkened room which was a perfect circle with an ascending stair climbing in a spiral at the edge.

'You haven't brought a light.'

'We won't need one.'

'We can't look at pictures without light,' Johnny said.

'They can be better in the dark,' she said.

In the middle of the round there was a stone case with an inscription that he couldn't read.

'This used to be the mausoleum. It contains my Grandfather. W wants to be buried here, surrounded by his art.'

Johnny smiled at the thought of Wollard anticipating his death in this way. Even Wollard had conceded his mortality and was clutching at comforts. He was afraid and he had channelled all his fears and doubts into this place, sought some solace in the art here and in some way decided that it was going to help him overcome death.

'The pictures run in order of acquisition. It makes it seem like a more personal collection, I think.'

He could see three black oblongs, just distinguishable as the Friedmans from Wollard's office, at the start of the collection.

'These were before Stephen went figurative.'

She continued to give critiques of the obscured Friedmans, Pockets, Le Shards and Daniels, as though finding them more interesting than anything, including Johnny.

'*Death in the Forest*,' she said. 'You must know it. The dog represents the artist, the forest is death. Every painting has some connection with death. It's my brother's little obsession.'

There was a rushing of blood in his ears and the incessant voice telling him that all this could be his.

'Are you all right?' Diane asked him.

'I am fine,' he said.

'You have to see all of them. Particularly the last.'

As they came to the last painting Diane paused and looked at him in anticipation of his reaction. She remained looking at him, not the painting, like someone who had presented a gift and could not wait for the recipient to open it.

He recognized the form and outline immediately and upon seeing Him he put his face up close. But in the dark it was hard to see the details of the face or discern the expression.

'The church didn't know what a valuable thing they had,' she said. 'W insisted that I keep it a secret. It's the original Smiling Icon of Ruban. The press don't even know about it yet.'

Johnny said nothing. He rummaged through his jacket pocket for the lighter that Penny had bought him.

193

'Careful,' Diane said as he flicked the flame and held it to the painting. 'You might catch the wood.'

He held the lighter above his head ducking under its tapering light, holding the trigger down until it burnt his thumb.

'Damn it. Can you hold it, just here?' he said.

Diane held the lighter for him and flicked the flame on and he squinted to look at the inscription and the frame to see that it was the same, the one, and then he looked at the face itself but the lighter kept overheating, forcing Diane to let go of the catch.

'It's almost priceless,' she reassured him. 'There's a remarkable use of gold leaf in the hair. You might just be able to make it out.'

'Just keep it on for another few seconds,' he said, not hearing her at all now. He cared little for the refinements and textures and schools she mentioned. It may have been a priceless work of art but it had its own intrinsic value to him. She had knowledge about it; he, for a moment, had a terrible understanding.

She let it cool and then flicked it again but the flame was getting low. He squinted in and looked at the eyes and for the mouth and in particular at the curve of the mouth but he could not tell if He was smiling or not. Then the flame died out again.

He took the lighter from her hand and shook it hard to get the fuel going and then he held the catch down for as long as he could, ignoring the burning of his thumb from the hot metal. He managed to keep the flame up for several seconds but when he looked at the image there was no longer enough light to see Him by.